The

Third

Season

By the Same Author

Novels

Wagons in the Wind
Three Across Texas
Three Across Kansas
Three Across Wyoming

Novella

The Siege of Canton

Nonfiction

Manual of Professional Remodeling
Spec Builder's Guide
Handbook of Construction Contracting, Vol. 1
Handbook of Construction Contracting, Vol .2
Remodeling Kitchens & Baths
Builder's Guide to Room Additions
Creating Space Without Adding On
Small Space/Big Bucks
House Framing
Garages & Carports

The

Third

Season

Jack P. Jones

GoldenIsle Publishers
Eastman, GA 31023

GoldenIsle Publishers
2395 Hawkinsville Hwy
Eastman, GA 31023

Library of Congress Catalog Card Number: 98-93595

Jack P. Jones, 1928-
 The Third Season / Jack P. Jones

ISBN 0-9666721-4-3

 1. Family ties - contemporary fiction. 2. Drug culture - effects – fiction.   3. Georgia - fiction. 4. Georgia swampland - mysterious.
I. Title
  II Title: The Third Season

Designed by Tena Ryals

Printed in the United States of America

First Edition

10 9 8 7 6 5 4 3 2

For the five-year-olds

They bounce into each new dawn
With a brilliant insight and a new
Wisdom, shattering the prim and
Exhaustive philosophy of the ages

Prologue

Some say that life is like the seasons: that spring brings life, summer gives growth and fall provides a harvest. But in the long, cold gray days of winter, all things die, or sink. They say it is in the third season when nature strokes its artistic brush that mankind is best revealed, for it is the time of grandchildren—the third generation.

Perhaps this is so. But, unlike the seasons of the year, which are, as it must be—cyclic, it is not so with man for the third season is always—always present. It is the only constant in the cycle of things. And, so should King Solomon have stated.

Chapter 1

Elmer Goodhand left the house, walking out to the lane leading off behind the barn and down by the cotton field. The girl, nearing five, slid off the porch swing and ran after him.

"Where are we going, Poppy?"

The old man grunted, saying she was being too inquisitive as always, and continued on, walking with a slight limp.

He preferred being alone, but Spice always ignored his wishes. That wasn't his granddaughter's name, but he'd always called her that. The man couldn't even remember why he'd given her the nickname except it seemed appropriate at the time.

She was more of a nuisance than anything else.

"Where are we going, Poppy?" She reached for his hand.

"Does it make any difference?"

"Naw," she said, looking up into his faded blue eyes. She shrugged. "It sounded nice to ask."

He mumbled something, wiping a handkerchief over his face. He kept hoping his daughter would return for Spice but knew that was doubtful. Elmer didn't even know where she'd gone. It had been almost five years now since she'd left. He didn't think much of a woman who'd dump a baby on someone and disappear.

"It might rain, Poppy."

He paused, straightening his shoulders as he looked up. A small cloud drifted across the sun. "Might someday."

"But, Poppy!"

He walked on, following a path through a growth of tall pines and into a clearing. "I know where we're going," said Spice. "It's to that old grave place."

He slowed his pace as they climbed the knoll. The girl, her short black hair bouncing in curls, skipped along.

Under the spreading oak, a single grave kept a lonely vigilance over a small brook. Sitting on the bench inside the fenced enclosure, he removed his hat, a wide-brim straw rendered shapeless by sun and rain.

"Poppy, you looking for God again?"

"Why'd you say that?"

"Because of what you said."

"What I said was that I had given up trying to find God because He's never around when you need Him."

"Poppy, you didn't say that! You said you'd give Him hell for letting grandma die if you ever saw Him."

The girl stood with hands on her hips. She was quickly outgrowing the overalls he'd not long ago bought her. Her green eyes narrowed as if she seriously disapproved of him. "You remember too much, girl."

She looked at the sky, sighing. "That's what you said!"

"There is no God," he said sharply.

"I know that."

"Grandma would have thought you a real sport, child," he said after awhile, looking down at the grave.

"I would have thought her a sport, too, wouldn't I?"

"Probably."

Elmer fanned with the hat. Strands of gray hair fell across his forehead. He wasn't a large man, not even overweight. When he was younger, he stood nearly six feet. Age had robbed him, he once thought, of a couple of inches and the mustache appeared whiter - and thicker - than his hair. His face was almost narrow, forming from a square jaw. Lucy, his deceased wife, had thought his eyes and expression too intense. "I wish you could have known your grandmother."

"Let's go, Poppy. I don't like this place."

"Then you should have stayed at the house."

"By myself!"

Elmer Goodhand studied his granddaughter. If her mother didn't soon come for her, he would contact the county to have her placed in a foster home or for adoption. He had to think of the child's future.

She reached for his hand. "I'm thirsty."

"You're either thirsty, hungry, wide awake, or sleepy - all at the wrong times."

She laughed. He thought she was a pretty child. "Oh, all right, we'll go. A little milk might do us both some good."

"I want ice tea."

"You'll drink what I drink."

Spice frowned.

He lifted her chin. "Or nothing."

"I'll drink what my Poppy does," the round face said.

Thunder rumbled in the southwest. "I told you," Spice said.

"Told me what?"

"That it's going to rain."

Slowly, he stood. "Now you're a weatherman."

"Yep."

"Tell you what, Spice. If it rains, I'll throw in some ice cream with that milk."

"Okay."

At the house he took the ice cream from the freezer and dipped out a scoop.

"Is *that* all I get?"

"It's a small shower, not a downpour."

"You didn't say it had to be a thunderstorm!" She stretched out both hands, piqued. He added another scoop to her dish. "Just don't ruin your supper."

"I won't."

The rain pelted the tin roof. He sat at the table reading the newspaper, not having anything else to do. He thought about driving into town. There were always some of his friends at the cafe. But, he'd have to take Spice, and it wouldn't be worth the trouble, so he contented himself scanning the paper and listening to the drone of the rain on the back porch roof.

"I thought you liked sitting on the front porch when it's raining, Poppy."

"I do."

Spice quickly finished the ice cream and left the table. "Then let's go sit, Poppy."

The rain came down harder. When he remodeled the old house, he'd extended the porch to the sides of the house. It was a comfort to be able to move with the shade or a breeze.

A bolt of forked lightning sizzled to the ground down at the edge of the swamp. Spice jumped from the swing and sat in the rocking chair near him. "Shouldn't we go inside?"

"It wasn't that close."

"I bet you Mr. House is glad it's raining," said Spice, rocking.

Elmer rented the four-hundred-acre farm to Bill House, a neighbor. The farm had its own irrigation system, but nothing could take the place of a soaking rain. Besides, irrigation was expensive to operate even when pumping water from a pond. The tobacco, cotton, and peanuts looked good. House might turn a decent profit if the weather continued favorably.

"How come you don't farm anymore, Poppy?"

"I grew tired of fighting drought, insects, and low prices."

"What's drought?"

"Dry weather."

"Now you build things, huh, Poppy?"

He reached out to slow her chair. "Careful, you'll tip over. Yeah, I build things. I like building things."

"You never built me a tree house."

"I don't climb trees anymore, either."

"I wish I had a tree house."

He lit his pipe.

"Smoking is bad for you, don't you know that?"

"Not as bad as a talkative young'un."

Spice stopped rocking to stare at him. "Poppy, if I don't talk, how do you know if I'm happy?"

"I could guess," he said, puffing on the uncooperative pipe.

He crossed his bad leg. "You know, there are some good, decent people who'd like to have a girl like you living with them."

The rocker stopped. "What do you mean?"

He didn't look at her. "I mean just that. You'd have a mother and a father to take care of you."

"You already take care of me."

"What if I should get sick?"

"Then I'll take care of you."

"What if I had to go into the hospital?"

"I'd go with you, Poppy; don't you know we're friends?"

He puffed on the pipe, feeling a small hand clasping his. Suddenly, she slid out of the chair. "I have to go to the bathroom."

"Be sure you turn off the light."

"Okay."

Why didn't his daughter write? He didn't know if she were alive or dead. A little girl needed a mother. How could Jo do this to him? What in the world could cause a woman to abandon her baby all these years? She had been raised to accept responsibility for her own actions.

His thoughts ran back over the years, wondering where he and Lucy might have made mistakes rearing their only child. Nothing came prominently to his mind. You'd think a woman with a good college education would have enough decency not to burden her father with a baby.

He had other interests in life. There were his books. He'd hardly had time to visit his study since Jo dumped Spice on him.

"Where you going, Poppy?"

"Up to my study."

"Can I go, too?"

"No." He paused midway up the stairs, looking back. Spice stood at the bottom of the wide stairway, hands thrust in the pockets, and her eyes glued to the floor.

"Oh, come on."

She bounded up the steps.

Books lined three walls of the large room. The surface of the desk he had so painstakingly made shone from its place near the large windows. He paused at the black leather chair with the brass tacks that Spice had promised herself she would count when she learned what came after seventeen. She propped herself in one of the two smaller chairs. "I like it in here, Poppy."

He grunted, wondering when he would ever again find the time to explore his books and spend a few quiet hours searching their treasures. When Lucy was alive, she would join him near the fireplace on winter nights to sit in silence with her sewing while he visited with Homer, the likes of Shakespeare, Hemingway, and Melville. On one shelf there were volumes about the Civil War. A series of books on the American west occupied another section. Near them Louis L'Amour works found a niche.

Elmer Goodhand had never been a selective reader. Any good writer captured his attention, whether the story had a western setting or took place on some New England coast. He'd read the King James Version of the Bible and was amazed at the beauty of the writings. That had been some years ago when Lucy was sick with cancer, when he had earnestly tried to find God. Failing in his search, he was left with his unanswered questions.

"I'm hungry, Poppy."

He looked longingly at a shelf of books he had planned to have already read. "Tell you what. I don't feel like cooking. It's too hot. Let's go to Shoney's."

"Okay."

The town of Action lay in Georgia's peanut and cotton country. Tall slash pines broke the monotony of end-on-end fields as oak, popular, sweetgum, and other like varieties crowded the damp places along the creeks and wet-weather rivulets. Cypress dominated the huge swamp.

Elmer liked the flat land. In the summer, gnats kept one's mind from dwelling on the heat and humidity. In the winter, the wind whispered through the pines, and quail hunters from up north brought in a few dollars. One Action merchant stated that those from out-of-state spent a hundred dollars for every quail bagged in the county.

An often overlooked asset of the county, Elmer often argued was the number of pretty girls one was likely to see in the high school. The boys were accustomed to this fact and often didn't appreciate its significance until they left the county for jobs or college. Their usual comment upon returning included, "You know something for a fact? There's some ugly women out there in this world!"

Thus, the county slogan: "Homegrown is best."

Action had always been home to Elmer. He was born and raised twenty miles from where he now lived. He had married one of the fair locals, and they had a pretty daughter who in turn had given birth in like measure. Had Jo's husband not died in a car accident, she might not have abandoned her child. She might have had more children and stayed in Action. The way it turned out, Elmer was glad Spice wasn't a twin.

At Shoney's, Elmer lifted Spice out of the truck. "Now, I want you to fill up. I don't want you calling for a midnight snack of eggs and bacon."

"I haven't done that since I was small," she replied.

"And you'll be drinking milk, young lady."

"How about some tea afterwards, okay?"

"Milk. Tea runs you to the bathroom all night."

Travelers from the nearby interstate highway crowded the restaurant. Elmer liked to say he'd done all his traveling at the expense of the army during the war. He didn't like to travel then and liked it even less now. Driving to Atlanta, he claimed, was a fast lane among idiots. The best thing he could say about the Atlanta experience was that no one had ever shot at him.

Spice made an excellent dining partner. Her table manners were due to his method of training. She looked the perfect lady, even with one of the overall galluses hanging off her shoulder. She had held her head out of the truck window, and her hair was a mess. One shoe was untied. Elmer didn't know how he'd missed those little details. Anyway, he didn't have to dine alone, a thing he hated because he never knew where one should look. He didn't like watching strangers eat. With Spice, that wasn't a problem. She glanced up, offering a wide smile.

"I finished my milk, Poppy. Can I have some tea now?"

"You were supposed to sip on it with your meal--not gulp it down all at once."

"You said drink milk, and I did. Can I have some tea?"

He summoned the waitress, and Spice received a large glass of tea with a slice of lemon riding the rim.

"Thank you, Poppy," she said, and the old man grunted.

Chapter 2

The old man packed tobacco in his pipe while the lawyer rambled. "You see, Elmer, I don't want this job botched," Rastus Wolfe cautioned, leading the way down the hall to a room designated as his library. "I've already spent a fortune trying to fix up this old place."

"This room's already botched," reminded Elmer.

"I know, I know," said the overweight attorney. "I need you to straighten it out."

Elmer surveyed the paneled room. He wondered how anyone doing such a poor job could call himself a carpenter. "It's like we discussed before. I work by the hour, and I get paid in cash -- fifteen dollars an hour."

"I can hire carpenters all day long for eight or ten bucks an hour, Elmer!"

"Is that what you paid the fellow who did this room? I've seen worse work but never in a house. Some farmer down the road from me built a cow shed that looked about like this mess."

"I guess I should have hired you in the first place."

"You were trying to save a few bucks, Rastus," Elmer had to say.

"How long will it take?"

"Don't know. Depends on how much I have to tear out."

"Make a guess!"

"Several weeks."

"Wha-at?!"

"You said make a guess."

"Elmer, I should report you to Social Security."

"Go ahead. I've never collected a dime from them."

"Well, you do know that you have to pay into it before you can take anything out."

Elmer nodded. He'd always believed he was better at handling his money than the government.

"And this cash business, Elmer. You ought to pay your share of taxes."

"I do--on everything except the few carpenter jobs I take on. When they stop wasting, I'll start paying on that, too."

Rastus placed a hand on Elmer's shoulder. "Make the raised panels like you did at the bank, Elmer. By the way, you ever decide what to do about your granddaughter?"

Elmer puffed on the pipe. "I've been thinking a foster home might be best in the interim."

"Want me to see what I can do? There are some reputable people in the county who'd love taking in a child like her."

"I'd rather she was placed out of the county. It'd be better on her not being so close by."

Rastus studied him. "You sure you want to part with her?"

"I'm thinking of her welfare," he said defensively.

"I'll put out some feelers then. I know the people at family services."

He was thinking of Spice's well-being, he told himself. The fact that she was a burden to him, taking up all his time, did not enter into it. The responsibility was too great. Like this morning, Mavis, who usually kept Spice when he was working a job, had to go to Macon for a doctor's appointment. That meant a search of the neighborhood to find someone to keep the child. He finally left her with the Lass family. They were fairly decent folk. The problem was Spice picked up curse words from the Lass kids. She'd be talking like a grammar school dropout by six o'clock.

The child needed a mother.

"When can you start this job?" Rastus wanted to know.

"I started an hour ago."

"You mean we've been standing round here chitchatting on my time?"

"That's right."

"You're the only person I know who gets fifteen dollars to say 'good morning.' "

"Lawyers get fifty."

Before picking up Spice, he drove out to the mall, searched through the children's racks at Wal-Mart, and purchased two pairs of overalls, one blue denim, one striped with a matching cap. Elmer didn't know the first thing about buying dresses. On the way to checkout, he selected a doll that caught his fancy. The large black-haired doll had on red overalls.

Spice threw her arms around his legs when he handed her the doll. "Damn, Poppy. She's pretty!"

He looked at Betty Lass. The woman shrugged. "They pick it up on TV."

Later, he had a long talk with Spice about word selection. Spice put on the striped overalls and cap. "The legs are too long," she advised.

"Roll 'em up."

"Where we gonna eat supper, Poppy?"

"Didn't Mrs. Lass feed you?"

"Some yukkies is all."

He started toward the kitchen.

"It's too hot for us to cook, Poppy. What's this tag doing on my back pocket?"

"Where you want to eat?"

"Smitty's."

"All they serve is hamburgers and fries."

"That's what I want."

He put on his hat, and they drove to Action. Smitty's wife swept Spice into her arms when they entered. "Here, let me remove this tag. You didn't steal these work clothes, did you?"

"I didn't steal them! Poppy bought them!"

At the booth, Spice whispered loudly, "Did you steal my overalls, Poppy?"

He frowned at her.

"I'm teasing; don't you know that?"

"Aren't you going to take off your cap?"

She shook her head. "I like it to stay right where it is."

A cool breeze swept up from the cornfield. The pecan trees surrounding the house gently rustled contentment. A whippoorwill repeated itself behind the house. Another one in the pines echoed back. Spice left the swing to curl up on his lap.

He lit his pipe and rocked.

An early moon peeked through the pines as the day faded.

"Mrs. Lass said there was a God, Poppy."

"Then may He rake some coals over their foul tongues."

"Mrs. Lass said God is a spirit. That's why we can't see Him."

He grunted.

"Poppy, how do you pray?"

"Where do you get such ideas?"

"Mrs. Lass said she prayed to God she wouldn't have to watch another repeat on TV."

"I think that is just a meaningless expression, Spice. If there is a God, He'd look with disfavor on Mrs. Lass' choice of words."

"Like He might push her mute button?"

"Yeah, I think He might do just that."

"I wish there were a God, Poppy. If there were, I'd ask Him to make you live forever."

The whippoorwill rehearsed again. The moon topped the pines. The breeze shifted. He carried the sleepy child into her bedroom adjoining his and put her down. She reached for her newest doll.

Going upstairs, he sat at the desk and refilled his pipe. Where had the years gone? Only yesterday Jo was the age of Spice. How had his life become so entangled with a child? She dominated all his time. Everything revolved around her needs. Where was *his* freedom?

There was only one option available to him -- find a good home for her with caring people.

The volume, *A Brief History of World War II,* lay on his desk. He abstractly turned the pages. He couldn't recall why he ordered the book. He'd fought in France and Germany. Reading about those engagements, as they were called, left him feeling that historians could be skimpy on facts and opinionated on causes. He decided not to read the book after all. The author had not even been born at the time. It was doubtful if he bothered to interview anyone who had personal knowledge of the "engagements."

He'd been wounded in France. A piece of shrapnel was dug out of his leg, and the following night he returned to the front line -- so much for recuperation and recovery. He had the U.S. Army to thank for a permanent limp. The shrapnel came from friendly fire.

Lately, Elmer was doing a lot of reflecting. Somehow, he couldn't recall much of anything he'd accomplished. Not that he'd ever hoped to do anything famous, but there should be more to life than sweat, toil, and disappointment. Look how many years it took him and Lucy to pay for the farm!

The farm, though, became his roots. It had been their life, and it had offered them a fairly comfortable living. It was good productive land. The big timber on the south one-hundred acres would bring a goodly amount if he decided to sell.

He would eventually need the money. At best, he only had a few good working years left. Perhaps he should save everything for Spice's education. God knows, it was getting expensive to learn two plus two anymore.

Why was he thinking like that? It wasn't his place to educate a grandchild. Let whoever adopted her foot the bill. Who said that everything he'd worked for would belong to a granddaughter?

"Poppy?"

She stood in the doorway. "I don't feel good."

When he lifted her, he felt the heat of her body. "Where do you hurt, child?"

"All over."

The glazed eyes and flushed face alarmed him. He carried her downstairs and out to the truck. "Where we going, Poppy?"

"Hospital."

"I don't want a needle shot." She leaned over in the seat, placing her head on his leg.

A young woman doctor examined Spice in the emergency room. Elmer had never seen her before. "Who's her physician?"

"Dr. Hall. He's been looking after her since she came into the world."

"I suggest you call him."

"What's wrong with her?"

"I don't know. We'll have to do some tests. Right now I want to get her fever down. Go make that call!"

Four hours later, Dr. Hall came from the Intensive Care Unit. Elmer had known the man for many years.

"She's a sick child, Elmer. We've managed to lower the fever a bit, and I hope we can keep it down."

"What's wrong with her, Doc?"

"Can't say just yet."

"Will she be all right?"

"Calm down, Elmer. We're doing everything we know to do."

"Dammit, is she going to be all right?"

"Elmer, how can I assure you when I don't know exactly what it is we're fighting here? It could be a virus of some kind. It might be something more serious."

"What's her temperature?"

"It's 105 right now."

He drew a quick breath. "You mean it was higher?"

"I'm afraid so."

"Doc, that could harm a person's brain!"

"I'm hoping she's out of the woods, Elmer. As for damage, we'll just have to wait and see. I've arranged to have her transferred to the children's hospital in Macon. We just don't have the facilities here."

Elmer followed the ambulance to Macon. Specialists were called in. Spice went into a coma. He couldn't believe a child so alive a few hours ago was attached to so many tubes and wires.

Leaning over the bed, he took her hand, his own shaking. She looked lifeless.

A nurse touched his arm. "I'm sorry. You must leave now."

He waited outside the unit for three days and four nights. The doctors remained uncertain about the nature of Spice's illness. More tests were being made. They advised him to go home; they would contact him as soon as there was a change.

"I'll stay. She'll want me when she comes around."

"Mr. Goodhand, when she rebounds, she'll need you rested and able to take care of her. Go home and get some rest."

He went home, but rest would not come. He began work on Rastus Wolfe's library. The lawyer advised that there was an out-of-county couple who would be happy to adopt Spice. "They're well-off. Own considerable property. Financially independent."

"I can't discuss it now, Rastus. We'll have to wait until she's recovered."

"Why are you working, anyway? Take some time off; why don't you?"

"I need to keep busy. Now get out of here and let me earn my money."

He packed his pipe and walked out onto the second level of the columnar porch. He dropped into a chair and abstractly lit the pipe.

Oh, God, are you there? Are you real? Help Spice if you exist!

That evening he bought a pony and saddle and had both delivered to the farm. Spice had said that was what she wanted for her birthday.

"You don't need a horse," he had told her.

"I know I don't need one, Poppy, but can't I *want* a horse?"

"How about a duck or rabbit?"

Placing hands on hips, she stared at him. "Do you know something, Poppy?"

"What?"

"You're just not making sense."

"How's that?"

"Because I'd look silly trying to ride a rabbit or a duck! I'm not *that* little."

"You want too much."

"My poppy will get me a horse, you'll see."

"Want to bet?"

"I don't have to."

He drove to Macon. In the unit, he looked at the comatose form in the tangle of hook-ups and tubes. "I bought you a horse, Spice," he mumbled. "A little spotted pony like you wanted."

The hospital chaplain found him in the waiting room. "I'm Jim Potts," he said, sitting in the chair near Elmer.

Elmer thought he looked too young for the job.

"I couldn't help but notice you listed no religious preference on the admission form."

"That why you're here?"

"No. I just wanted to offer my services; if there is anything I can do— "

"There isn't."

"She's certainly a beautiful child. I'm sure the nickname fits her."

"It does."

"I took the liberty of calling Dr. Hall. You weren't here at the time, so I could get your permission. I wanted to know something about her."

"That was all right."

"Mr. Goodhand, I'm praying that God in His wisdom will look after Spice."

"I appreciate your concern."

"If you don't object, I'd like to keep a check on her. I hope to be there when she comes around.

"Why?"

"To tell her that her grandpa is coming to see her. She'll be asking for you; you can be assured of that."

"Tell her -- tell her she has a pony and saddle at home."

"I'll be delighted to tell her that."

He stood to leave. "That's what she wanted for her birthday."

He limped out.

Chapter 3

The house felt strangely quiet. He stood in the doorway to Spice's room, feeling a heavy loneliness sweep over him. The doll in the red overalls lay on the floor where she'd dropped it the night she turned ill. He sat on her unmade bed, looking at the neat row of dolls on the window seat.

She had searched him out that night for help. She had no one else in the world to whom she could turn. That was the shame of it all.

He went out onto the porch and sat in a rocking chair. He didn't hear the whippoorwill nor notice the moon. Neither did the sound of the wind in the pecan trees register. All he could think about was Spice connected to tubes.

Except for him, the child was alone. How would she grow up in the ever increasing muck of decadence? How does innocence manage its fragility in such an environment? He knew, if she lived, he would have to do something with her, place her with a caring couple who could protect her.

If she lived . . .

His hands shook when he filled his pipe. The match glowed against the worried lines in his face. The medical bills would soon be coming due. Well, there was that stand of big trees. He'd never thought too much about why he was saving the timber, always viewed it as a reserve in case of an emergency. He would hate to see the massive trees cut. They were a link to the past when he and Lucy shared life. She was always fond of the tall pines.

"Those trees give us stability, Elmer," she'd said. "It's bad when folks rake the land clear for a dollar. I'd rather listen to the wind sweeping through tall pines than hear the rustle of money." And so the trees continued to grow even though at times they'd found it hard to stretch their money for necessities.

He heard the light wind whisper through the big timber. He puffed on his pipe.

"Poppy, when I get big, I want me a farm, too." Spice had said one afternoon while following him to the barn. "Don't you think that's a good idea?"

He grunted.

"Poppy, yes or no?"

"I'm thinking about it."

"You always take too long to think, Poppy."

Elmer mumbled something.

"You oughta think fast like me."

"That's the reason you get into so much trouble, gal."

"I'm a girl! And I'm in no trouble this minute, am I?"

"Don't think so."

"Well, it's a good thing I'm not because I haven't done anything wrong all day."

"You didn't make up your bed this morning."

"I did, too!"

"Sure didn't look like it to me, wrinkled the way it was."

"Well, I'm a *little* girl. When I'm bigger, I'll rub out the wrinkles."

"I suppose that explanation will keep you out of trouble for a while."

She smiled, "When do I get my dollar?"

"Dollar? For what?"

"For not being a troublemaker!"

"I already paid you for that a couple of days ago."

"I don't have the dollar."

"What happened to it?"

"I bought ice cream with it, remember?"

They entered the barn. "You can't spend your money on ice cream and expect to have it, too."

She tugged at his hand. "But, Poppy, I'm not supposed to pay for my ice cream. *You* are."

"Who says?"

"I do. Don't you know little girls with a poppy never have to pay for ice cream? You owe me a dollar, so hand it over."

He paused, looking through his wallet. "You were born with it, weren't you?"

"With what?"

"Never mind," he said, handing her the dollar. "My grandfather never gave me more'n a nickel at the time, and there were very few times."

"I know."

"How do you know?"

"Because you say that a lot."

"Then why don't you ask for nickels?"

"You can't buy much ice cream with an old nickel, Poppy. Don't you know that?"

Elmer arrived at the Wolfe house early to begin a day of hard activity. Being engaged in productive labor refreshed his mind and body. He needed work. He needed to keep busy when he was troubled.

During the week he put in long hours at the lawyer's house, and at the end of the day drove to Macon to see Spice. There would be no change in her condition, and he'd return home confused, wondering why fate was so cruel to his granddaughter.

The doctors admitted they didn't know what was wrong with Spice. Her illness remained a mystery to them. Only the young chaplain seemed positive about the outcome. Elmer thought him foolish.

Fate stunk. Life became a stench. It was a struggle from the day you were born until the day death blundered through the door. One planned and worked to feed and educate his offspring, and little, if anything, ever turned out like you hoped it would.

There was just too much bad that could happen to a person. Everywhere you turned there was something that would get you. What had Spice ever done to deserve such a sickness? What foolish higher power, if there were such a thing, would let little ones suffer such tragedy?

Don't talk to Elmer Goodhand about God. No, sir. What little he'd achieved in life he'd earned with his own sweat and two hands. God didn't have anything to do with it. God didn't plow a single furrow nor drive so much as one nail for him.

A chain of frogs performed down at the small creek below the barns. Crickets sawed away in the yard.

"You know what, Poppy?"

"What?" He'd asked, recalling an evening on the porch only a few days ago.

"I'd sure like to see my mother."

So would I, he thought. "Maybe someday she'll come back."

"Do you really think so?"

"She might."

Spice sat in the chair near him, rocking it to the limit of balance. "I don't think she loves me."

He didn't attempt an explanation. He'd long ago run out of excuses for Jo.

"Poppy, when are you gonna buy me a dress anyway?"

"What's wrong with overalls?"

"Nothing."

"Dresses are expensive."

"Then save some money, Poppy. Don't you know anything?"

"We may have to cut down on the ice cream and cookies to save enough the way you wear out clothes."

Spice stopped rocking. "I don't think I want you to save money *that* way."

"I suppose you want me to quit buying pipe tobacco?"

She resumed rocking. "Yep. You could do that."

The next morning Elmer found Janet Wolfe, the lawyer's wife, waiting for him in the unfinished library.

"Did my husband mention that I wanted the windows overlooking the balcony enlarged?"

Elmer briefly studied the woman. He'd heard she usually spent summers with her family in Michigan. "He never mentioned it."

She sighed. Elmer wondered what a young woman of her looks saw in Rastus Wolfe. With a swing of her head, the long blonde hair fell neatly in place over her shoulders. "I want the windows enlarged to twice their present width."

She looked at him, but he didn't think she really saw him.

"Lady, I'm not going to do anything to those windows. They're fine the way they are."

"Pardon?" She was seeing him now.

Elmer packed his pipe. He could tell he was beginning to infuriate her.

"Well, think about it. If I enlarge those windows, you'll ruin the appearance of the house."

"Are you--"

"This old house was designed in the colonial era. Fact is, we call it a colonial mansion for lack of a more specific nomenclature."

"I know Southern history!"

"No one in his right mind would put modern windows in a place like this."

"Are you finished, Mr. Goodhand?"

"I am except to say I'm not about to ruin a fine old antebellum mansion with outrageous windows!"

She swung her head again. "You're *working* for us!"

"Rastus hired me to rework this room, that's right."

"Are you refusing to do as you're instructed?"

"I'm refusing to tinker with tradition."

She tried staring him down. "My husband will hear of this. I always heard you were difficult to work with, Goodhand."

"I bet young Yeager at the bank told you that."

"No. His father did."

"Well, neither of those Yeagers has much sense for form. With folks like that, you have to do the work right regardless of their crazy ideas."

"You're impossible!"

He lit the pipe, nodding. "I suppose so."

"Have you ever been fired from a job, Goodhand?"

"Sure have."

She stepped over pieces of molding. "Well, you're about to be fired from this one, too. I'm going to tell my husband exactly what you said."

"Tell him we need a better grade of crown molding while you're at it. This stuff they sent over isn't fit for a barn."

She stomped sawdust off her feet, mumbling.

Before noon the crown molding arrived. A few minutes later Rastus Wolfe stuck his head in the doorway. "It's looking good Elmer."

"Your wife was a mite upset when she left. Guess you heard."

The lawyer chuckled. "I'm glad you set her straight about the windows. She never listens to me."

Elmer grunted, coming down off the ladder. "You need taller shelves on the other wall. Give the room more balance."

"Fine. Go ahead with it."

"Don't you want to know what I have in mind?"

"I trust your judgment."

Rastus Wolfe walked through the room. "I think we've got a lead on the whereabouts of your daughter, Elmer."

Chapter 4

"She's in California, in a prison," the lawyer explained, following Elmer out onto the porch. "She's being released next month."

Elmer knocked ashes from his pipe. "What'd she do?"

"It concerned drugs--cocaine. According to the investigator's report, she was involved with a dealer. He's also getting out."

Elmer put the pipe away. "Think I'll call it a day, Rastus."

"There's something you should consider, Elmer. They could come here. She might even want the child back, if the girl recovers."

Elmer nodded, looking out across the wide yard. Pulling on his straw hat, he turned to the lawyer. "It never stops pouring, does it?"

"Sometimes, it sure looks that way."

Later, when the sun neared its trip's end, Elmer left his study and walked to the grave on the knoll.

"I'm in a tangle, Lucy," he said aloud. "Since you left, nothing ever goes right anymore. Remember how you used to run on about my not being the heathen I held out to be. I never claimed to be a heathen, Lucy. I just couldn't believe in a higher being the way you did. If your God exists, then why are you there and Spice near death? She might be brain-dead for all the doctors know."

He bent down, pulling a weed growing near the monument. "What's your God doing, Lucy? Playing poker with the devil? Jo went bad, Lucy. She took up dope and is in prison. We sure did it all wrong, honey. I thought we were raising her right. I guess we failed."

He sat on the bench. "The way I see it, there's not much hope for Jo or Spice. Jo knew better. She has only herself to blame."

He wiped away the perspiration. "I'm worried about Spice, honey. She deserves better. Tell that to your God. Tell Him I'm holding Him responsible if Spice doesn't make it, you hear? I'm not saying He exists; but if He does, I've about had it with Him. If He's in control like some folks claim, then He's mighty sloppy about a lot of things."

Putting on his hat, he shook his head. "Ain't a damn thing in this life makes sense anymore. I'm just tired of it. I'm tired of fighting every day, Lucy."

When he reached the house, he changed into a dry shirt, turned on the air conditioner, and went upstairs to the study. Taking a ledger from the desk, he opened a journal he'd labeled *Personal Observations*.

He wrote:

Giving way to defeatism would be easy considering the situation. As old as I am, I should have greater wisdom, more knowledge, and more control over events affecting me. Man, I am able to surmise from the experience of years, controls little more than his daydreams.

Though I have always read a great deal, I've discovered only a few capable of expressing a particular wisdom in an intelligent and cohesive way. I have, however, found that children have a talent for explaining in few words nuggets of treasures that puts to shame the so-called great philosophers. It has occurred to me that the greater minds are in small heads and that most of the deep thinkers lose it by school age. This is a great mystery to me.

This brings me to you, Spice, should you ever read these pages. I am at a loss to explain my feelings concerning you at this moment. You are fighting death, and my whole being is numb from worry. I've often been accused of being hardheaded and cantankerous, with little emotions. That's not true. I'm just not the outgoing type. What I feel, I feel, and I prefer to let it flow slowly outwardly so as not to overburden the object. A sudden outburst of sunshine can wilt a flower. I am saying that what is natural for me might be odd or strange for others. But note that pretense is the cheapest form of self-indulgence.

You mean more to me than I can tell you. You've filled an old man's life with a trail of beautiful gems. At times you've been both a trial and a delight. Having you always underfoot is both taxing and joyful. You always win the arguments even when I'm forced to constrain your little nose to a far, far corner. How you manage to manipulate your much wiser (?) grandfather at every turn of the road is an experience in itself. I see much of your grandmother in you.

Your well-being and future care is of utmost importance. That is why I must decide what is the best alternative. At present, I feel it would be best to place you under the care of a couple who would love you and see to your proper upbringing. Your needs and education won't be a problem where money is concerned. I have arranged for all my property to be held in trust for that purpose.

He closed the book and went out to the porch. Moon-made shadows stretched across the yard. A breeze from the south brought more humidity. Down among the tall pines, the whippoorwill took to calling. Swamp dogs sounded far off in the swamp. In the far field an irrigation pump started, its monotonous hum a disturbance.

He sat in a rocking chair, the aroma of pipe tobacco hanging in the air. When the pickup turned into the drive, he grunted. The truck braked to a quick stop. The woman, wearing a print dress and a man's straw hat, came up the steps carrying a basket.

"Elmer, you don't have a lick of social consciousness. Why didn't you tell me Spice was in the hospital?"

She placed the basket on the round table between the rocking chairs and sat down, fanning with the hat. "Is it hot!"

Mavis Hornberry, a widow going on three years, was in her early sixties. She was grayer and heavier than she admitted.

"Nothing you could have done," said Elmer.

"Friends keep friends posted."

Elmer couldn't think of a suitable reply.

"Stop your grunting. You sound like a hog in a wallow. You got any tea made?"

"Might be some in the refrigerator."

She went inside, returning with two glasses filled with ice. "I knew you wouldn't have any made." She took a plastic milk jug from the basket and filled the glasses.

She fixed his plate with fried chicken, pork and beans, and potato salad. Mavis had even thought to bring cloth napkins, one of which she'd tucked in his collar.

"You shouldn't have gone to so much trouble, Mavis."

She gestured with a drumstick. "Your problem is you don't know when you need help, Elmer Goodhand."

"I can cook."

"That's not what I'm talking about."

He swallowed cold tea and sampled the potato salad.

Mavis reached for a second piece of chicken. "Lucy was my friend, and I expect you to let me know when anything happens out here. Elmer, I wanted you to have a decent meal, and to find out what I can do for Spice. I can even spend some time with her at the hospital."

"She wouldn't know you were there."

"I feel like I need to do something."

He tried the beans. "All that can be done is being done."

"What about when you bring her home?"

"I'll manage."

"Sure you will. You'll be tied to the house, and I know how much you hate that. I'll come over and stay awhile."

"You want that last piece of chicken?" he asked.

"No, you eat it. When are you going to put in my new sink?"

"I told you I don't do plumbing."

"You did yours."

"That's different. I'm not paying a plumber thirty dollars just to drive out here."

"And I should!"

"You live in town. They wouldn't charge you that much. With the trouble you're always having with your pipes, you should marry a plumber."

"I was married to a painter, and I never could get that man to lift a brush at home. Elmer, you handymen are all alike. Look at that bottom step!"

"I'll fix it when I get around to it."

"That's what my husband used to say, too."

She cleaned off the table and packed the basket. "I heard they located Jo."

"Where'd you hear that?"

"From a cousin who is a sister-in-law to one of the clerks in Rastus' office."

"I guess the whole town knows by now."

"Probably. What will you do if she comes for Spice?"

"She doesn't want Spice. Never did."

"She might have had a change of heart, Elmer."

He took out his pipe. "Spice is her daughter. I reckon I couldn't stop her if she wanted her back."

"I don't believe you, Elmer Goodhand!"

"I might not have any say in the matter."

"You sound as if you'd like to get rid of the child."

"Thanks for the supper, Mavis. I appreciate it."

On the drive to Macon he wondered what he would do if Jo came for Spice.

He stood over the bed wishing there was something he could do for his granddaughter. Spice still looked like death. The chaplain came to stand beside him.

"Why?" Elmer muttered.

"That's one of the unanswerable questions, Mr. Goodhand. Only God knows."

"They don't even know what's wrong with her. All the tests turned out negative. How can they treat her if they don't know what's making her sick?"

The young chaplain shook his head.

Elmer spent silent minutes looking down at the sallow face. When he left the unit, the chaplain was waiting in the hall. "You look tired, Mr. Goodhand. Wouldn't you like a cup of coffee before starting home?"

"I'm fine, thanks."

"Don't give up on Spice. I'm sure that little girl has a lot of spunk left in her."

"She does," he said, turning down the hall. "But it might not be enough."

On the morning of the twenty-first day of Spice's hospitalization, the chaplain called Elmer. "Spice is awake. She wants to see her poppy," the broken voice said.

Elmer sat at the kitchen table, his hands shaking. Tears filled his eyes. He tolerated this for only a moment, wiped his face and stood up, holding himself erect. "Well, the little dickens! Guess I'd better put on a suit and go see about her."

Spice sat on the edge of the bed eating ice cream. "Hi, Poppy. What took you so long? And your clothes are all dirty."

With the chaplain looking on, Elmer knelt at the bed and hugged his granddaughter. "I had a flat tire," he said.

Chapter 5

Three days later, he carried Spice home. Mavis Hornberrry had already moved into the back bedroom and busied herself setting the house in order, according to her ideas.

"I want to see my pony," Spice said, getting out of the truck.

"I'll bring him up to the house, " Elmer said. "I don't want you out in the sun just yet."

So, for a week, Elmer tied the pony in the yard, and Spice admired him from the shade of the porch. Afterwards, Elmer spent a greater part of his time leading the pony around the yard with Spice in the saddle until he was satisfied that neither girl nor pony presented a hazard. Mavis, in the meantime, kept them overly fed and mothered to the point that both Elmer and Spice breathed a sigh of relief when she decided it was safe to leave them to their own ways.

Elmer and Spice sat on the shady side of the house rocking in the cool of the evening. "Know what, Poppy?"

"What?"

"I don't like this dress Mrs. Hornberry bought me."

"If you don't like the dress, go put on a pair of your overalls."

She disappeared into the house. She returned wearing striped overalls. "I feel better," she announced, climbing into the rocking chair. "When are you going to buy me some shorts?"

"I can't picture you wearing shorts with those cowboy boots."

"These are *cowgirl* boots, Poppy. Do you think Spotty misses me?"

"He's right out there grazing under a tree. I don't see how he could be missing you when he can see you sitting right here."

"I like my pony."

"You should. He cost enough."

"Of course, he did. You don't think a pretty pony like him is cheap, do you?"

As the darkness drifted in, Spice left her chair to climb onto his lap. Elmer rocked her to sleep. He put her to bed, removed the boots, and returned to the porch with a cup of coffee.

The serenade of the whippoorwill began beyond the fields. The words of the chaplain came to his mind. "I believe all healing comes from God. Perhaps we've just witnessed a miracle here. Who knows? I choose to believe the hand of God lifted up your granddaughter. I've been praying for a miracle."

Elmer didn't know what to think. The doctors certainly didn't do much. You'd think they would be embarrassed to charge such exorbitant fees for doing so little. He had to sell a section of the big timber to pay the medical bills. All during the day the chainsaws screamed the downfall of his majestic pines.

Mavis came out to care for Spice while he worked on the lawyer's library. Janet Wolfe was at the house every day supervising the three painters working downstairs. She frequently came upstairs to inspect his work. One Monday afternoon she brought him a glass of tea and a slice of cake.

"You are really good at what you do, Mr. Goodhand," she said pleasantly. She wore black shorts and a white blouse. Elmer thought she had a fine figure.

"I try to do good work."

"I wish the painters were as dedicated as you are."

He swallowed tea. "Painters are a strange lot."

"Meaning?"

"A lot of them are strange."

"They say the same thing about carpenters."

He measured a board. "I suppose that's the truth, too."

"Most men your age are retired."

"Most men my age are dead."

"Rastus said you read a lot. Is that true?"

He nailed the board in place. "I used to."

"Meaning, before you started taking care of your granddaughter?"

"Something like that."

"I'm just getting around to reading *Gone With the Wind*," she said. "I find it fascinating."

He wiped a large blue handkerchief over his face. "I've read it twice; it's about as close to being the great American novel as we'll ever get."

"Well, I wouldn't go that far."

"How could you? You haven't read it yet."

She shrugged, flipping her hair. "I've often thought about writing a novel."

He finished the glass of tea. "You wouldn't have a refill on this, would you?"

"Certainly. I'll bring up the pitcher if the painters left any."

She returned with the pitcher and filled his glass. "I did start a romance story once but gave it up. One could hardly get any recognition with that sort of thing."

He tasted the tea. "Seems to me you should write what appeals to you, not what the critics might think."

"Have you ever thought about writing, Mr. Goodhand?"

"Once. I'd planned to take Hemingway's place, but I never had the time to jot down anything."

She laughed. "I mean, seriously."

He shook his head. "What would an old farmer have to say that anyone would care to read?"

"Perhaps a western, or would that be beneath you?"

"Yeah, I wouldn't want to write undignified stuff like *Lonesome Dove*. It's not the locale or period. It's the talent that makes a book. If I had any writing talent, I'd probably do something with a farm background. It's all I know."

"I look forward to visiting with you again, Mr. Goodhand," she said, starting for the door.

"That'd be fine with me. I don't often get to talk with a pretty woman."

A smile touched her face. "What happened to the gruffy old man?"

"He left with the smart Yankee gal."

By the weekend, he'd completed the library and drove to the other side of Action to discuss remodeling a kitchen. Honest Billy Bob Brewster stood six feet and three inches and looked to Elmer to be ten months pregnant. He'd seen Billy Bob's used car commercials on television. He once did a commercial wearing a John Wayne look-alike outfit while sitting astride a donkey. The man's loud voice came across as scratchy and irritating. It was the same in person, only more so.

"The little wife wants a top-notch job with all the latest," informed Billy Bob. "We don't want no second-rate stuff. I paid big bucks for this hacienda, and we've got to keep things in perspective."

"Yeah," said Elmer.

"I don't mind paying top dollar so long as I get quality work," said Billy Bob.

"Yeah."

"I want a first class job here, Pop."

Elmer grunted, reaching for his pipe. He followed Billy Bob around the kitchen, mentally noting that everything the man suggested represented bad taste.

"Ever see me on TV, Pop?"

"The name's Elmer."

Billy Bob looked down at him. "Sure. Whatcha think of my TV commercials?"

"They're good for your competitors."

Billy Bob laughed, slapping Elmer on the back. "I'm selling cars, Elmer. I'm selling cars!"

"Yeah."

"Now whatcha think? My ideas for the kitchen good or bad?"

"Bad."

Billy Bob hitched up his pants. "So, what do you recommend?"

Elmer lit his pipe. He expressed his opinion on each item in the order Billy Bob had mentioned.

"Okay, okay, you get with the little woman and you two work it out. How do you work? Contract or by the hour?"

"By the hour."

"How much?"

Elmer gave himself a sizeable raise.

The car dealer whistled. "Man, you're expensive. I didn't realize nail drivers raked in that kind of dough."

"The good ones do."

"Okay, but it had better be professional."

"I get paid every Friday," informed Elmer.

"Sure thing. Man, I'm gonna have to unload some buggies to pay you."

The "little woman" turned out to be a pleasant relief. "Ignore Billy Bob," advised June Brewster, a tall, slender woman in her mid-thirties. "He's a big mouth."

"Uh, huh," agreed Elmer.

"What I want is exactly what I overheard you telling my husband. Could we go with stainless steel appliances, though?"

"Stainless steel will work fine."

He wouldn't have taken the job except he wanted to stay busy. He didn't want to sit around the house worrying if Jo would come or what she might have planned concerning Spice.

"Know something, Spice?" he said to the girl late Saturday afternoon.

"What?"

"I'd like some fresh fish for supper, how about it?"

"Okay."

"Think you can help me catch some?"

"Probably yes. Probably no."

"I see. That certain, huh?"

She nodded.

Near sundown, he drove the truck to the ten-acre pond on the backside of the farm where the dense swamp joined his property. Here was a place Lucy had loved. She preferred fishing in the spring or fall when the evenings were cooler.

Handing Spice her straw hat, he led the way down the bank to the boat. He carried his favorite rod and reel. Spice held onto her small rig.

He rowed over to where trees shaded the water, keeping near the banks where the water remained shallow. "You want to fish with crickets, worms, or what?"

"A 'what' sounds better."

He baited her hook with a cricket. "It's a nice fat bug," he advised.

"Yuk!"

With the third try, Spice landed the cricket in the water.

"You're dangerous with that thing," Elmer said, ducking the throw.

"Well, you taught me, Poppy."

"Why is it that when things go wrong, it's because I taught you?"

She shrugged. "I guess that's the way it is."

"You like to fish, don't you?"

"I like being with my poppy."

He pulled the hat brim down to shade his eyes and lit his pipe. He cast the black plastic worm near the top of a pine that had blown into the pond.

"I'm thirsty, Poppy."

Opening the small ice chest, he withdrew a plastic jug and poured her a cup of milk.

"I want a Coke."

"Sorry, all I have is milk and water."

She frowned, reaching for the cup. Taking a sip, she placed the cup between her knees. "Coke would have been better; you know that, Poppy?"

"Not for little girls, it isn't."

"I'll be glad when I'm growed up," she muttered.

"Looks like something sunk your cork."

Spice jerked the rod. "I got one!" she screamed. "It's a big one, too!"

"Play him easy, now."

He watched her struggle with the fish, cranking the reel.

"Ain't you going to help me?"

"You're doing just fine."

"I might lose my fish!"

"There's others."

She finally managed to bring the bream to the boat. He reached for the line and pulled in the fish. "Looks like you've caught your supper, girl."

"I can eat more'n one little fish, Poppy."

He put a fresh cricket on for her. "Better catch another then."

She soon caught one. "That's two for me. I don't think you're doing too good, Poppy."

"How can I when I spend all my time baiting your hook and taking off your catch?"

She giggled. "It's okay, Poppy. I'll let you have one of my fish."

He hooked a large mouth bass. The fish leaped out of the water, making a big splash.

"Damn, what a fish, Poppy! Don't let him get away!"

He glanced at her. "Watch your words, young lady," he said sharply.

He played the five-pounder.

"I think I'll eat that one," Spice said seriously.

"I'll give you half of him - once he's caught."

"Okay."

Later, a large bream tugged on Spice's line. It became a tug of war. Spice grunted. The rod bent a loop as the fish charged in an opposite direction.

Tongue out, she held on, beads of perspiration forming on her forehead. She looked at him. "Poppy, you just can't sit there! I need help!"

"You're doing just fine."

"How do you know?"

"He hasn't pulled you into the pond yet."

"If he does, you'll be sorry." She switched tongue to the other cheek.

"Not half as much as you will."

She frowned. "You're supposed to help little people!"

"Keep winding "

She grunted under the strain, pulling, and winding. When the fish dashed near the boat, she gave a hard pull on the rod. The fish sailed out of the water, flying over her head and off the hook. Spice threw down the rod. "See what you made me do. I lost him!"

He looked at the pouting face. "Fisherman's luck."

"Damn Poppy luck!" She folded her arms, staring across the pond.

The pout passed quickly. He baited the hook and handed her the rod. She flipped the bait in the water with renewed energy. "You know what?"

He grunted.

"You're not supposed to let me do all the work."

"That's true. Are you getting tired?"

"A little, I guess."

"We'll go in if you like. We have plenty for supper."

"Wait 'til I catch one more."

She caught one more and then another before she was ready to quit. "I'm a good fisher, ain't I?"

"You sure are."

"I caught more than you did, didn't I?"

"You did. You always do."

She ran to the truck. "Hurry up, Poppy. I'm hungry."

A red sports car was parked in the yard. He saw his daughter sitting on the porch.

Chapter 6

The thirty-year-old woman wore faded denim jeans and an off-white blouse. Elmer thought she had on too much makeup. Dark brown hair hung straight over her shoulders. The hazel eyes lacked spark. The round face had a hollow look.

"It's good to see you, Dad," she greeted.

Stepping back, Jo looked down at Spice. "I would never have recognized her."

"She was only a week old when you left."

She knelt down in front of Spice. "Should I tell her?"

"I know who you are," Spice said, stepping back and reaching an arm around Elmer's leg. "Poppy showed me your pictures."

Jo made no effort to take her. Spice held onto Elmer. Jo stood, taking in the farm with a sweep of her hand. "Nothing's changed."

"I'll put the fish on ice, and we'll talk," he offered.

"I can't stay long, Dad."

"Come on into the kitchen out of the heat."

He listened quietly as she made small talk. Drinking coffee, Jo lit one cigarette after the other. Spice watched television in the den.

"I know you just got out of prison," he said after awhile, not looking at her.

She nodded. "Gus told me you hired a private investigator to look for me."

"Why didn't you ever write, Jo? Weren't you even curious about Spice?"

"Spice? Is that what you call her?" She seemed perturbed. "What was wrong with the name I gave her?"

"Nothing. Lucy is a fine name. Your mother would've been proud to have a granddaughter named after her."

Jo lit another cigarette. "I really don't like Spice as a nickname."

"What have *you* called her these past years?"

She stood. "Well, I'm here to take her off your hands."

"And go where?"

"We don't know yet. Gus has been talking about a trip to Florida. Thinks he'd like to spend a few weeks with some friends. Then maybe we'll spend some time in Atlanta." She shrugged. "We have no definite plans."

"I think you do. Sounds like you plan to do some dope running. Whose car are you driving?"

"It belongs to Gus. Why?"

"You want Spice to take along on your travels. Arouse less suspicion with a kid along, wouldn't it?"

"She's my daughter!"

"And you're mine. Break away from that crowd and stay here. Get to know Spice. Give her time to get acquainted with you."

"I love Gus."

"He's a dope peddler and a hood!"

"He's a businessman!"

"A business that'll send you both back to prison."

"They set him up before."

"They?"

"Some people in Miami."

"And next time some people in Atlanta will set him down. Maybe you, too. You're in the wrong crowd, Jo. Don't you care anymore?"

"Like I said, I love him. Besides, you're assuming a whole lot."

"You can't take Spice with you."

She went to the sink, pressing the cigarette out in the drain. "Dad, don't oppose Gus. He can be unpleasant."

"Is he forcing you to go with him?"

"No. It's like I told you. We're, well, we're living together. He wants me to have my daughter."

He knocked ashes from the pipe. "She stays here."

"Dad, you don't know Gus. He's a great guy but he--well, he does have a temper."

"Isn't he the same Gus you knew in high school? Shorty Smith's youngest boy as I recall."

"Yes, he's the one. You never did like the Smiths, did you?"

"And for good reason. I don't like trash."

"Look, let me take my kid for a couple of months. If it doesn't work out, I'll bring her back."

He searched her eyes. She looked away. "You'd use her for some hood's gain?"

She produced another cigarette. "I see I still can't talk to you."

"You can stay here and get acquainted with your daughter. She's not leaving here. Not for a long while," he said flatly.

"I could never stay here. I always hated the country."

"It's better than prison."

She lit the cigarette. "I'll be going now. I don't know how Gus is going to take this."

"Jo, my concern is for that little girl in there. I'll protect her if it means having you and your crooked friend locked up."

Jo rushed out of the house. Elmer sat at the table, resting his head on his hands. His daughter hadn't changed. The child meant nothing to her.

She had duly warned him. Gus could be mean if he didn't get his way. He picked up the telephone and dialed Rastus Wolfe's home.

"Look, Elmer," the lawyer said after Elmer had explained Jo's visit. "If Jo takes her child, I don't know if there's anything we can do about it. It's not like kidnapping, you know. She is the mother."

"What about the reason they want her?"

"That's your assumption, Elmer."

"I'm not letting her have Spice."

"You might not be able to prevent it. She can enter your house and get her. How would you be able to stop them?"

"What about getting the sheriff out here?"

"For what? No crime has been committed."

"Suppose they break into my house and take her?"

"Then it might be a matter for the courts, and that'll take time for whatever good it'll do."

"I'm not letting them take her, Rastus."

"Look, let me think."

Elmer waited.

"Elmer, you know that cabin of mine down on the river?"

"I know where it is."

"Take the kid and stay there until you hear from me. Keep out of sight."

"Jo knows about the cabin. It'd be the first place they'd look. If I've got to hide out, I'd rather do it in the swamp joining my place."

"With a kid? You're too old to be going into a place like that!"

"All I need are a few provisions. You forget, I used to hunt and fish that swamp."

"And so did the Smiths. Gus was practically raised in that place; have you forgotten?"

"I'll take my chances."

"I wouldn't, Elmer. Not with a kid."

"It's better than the alternatives."

"How can I get in touch with you?"

"You can't."

"Elmer, if something happened to you in there, we'd never find you or the girl."

He hung up the telephone. Getting the 30-30 Winchester out of the closet, he buckled on a cartridge belt, found his large pocketknife, and hurriedly threw cans of food into a canvas bag.

At the barn, he found the tarpaulin. He rolled the canvas and put it in the back of the truck. Hurrying back inside, he gathered the clothes he and Spice would need. He switched off the television set. "Let's go camping, Spice."

"Okay."

As Elmer turned off the lane through the woods, the headlights of an approaching car swept the night sky. He switched off the engine. The red sports car roared up the driveway.

"We're hiding from them, Spice, so don't make any noise."

"Are you going to shoot them?"

"Certainly not."

He waited. They'd had plenty of time to search the house. Gus might realize they'd not left the farm and come searching for them.

"We have to do some walking, honey."

Quietly, he gathered the tarpaulin, the bag of provisions, and clothes. He handed Spice a small tote bag. "Can you carry that for a while?"

"Yep."

"We can't use a flashlight, so stay close behind me and don't talk."

"Okay, Poppy."

In a few minutes they were at the edge of the swamp. Looking back, he saw the headlights approach where he parked the truck. "Hey, old man," called Gus. "I don't want to hurt you, so give up the kid and we'll be on our way."

"Poppy, don't give me away!"

"They're not getting you, honey."

"Come on, Pop," Gus yelled. "Don't make me lose my patience, man! Come daylight, I'll find you."

Gus cursed. "I'll hurt you, old man. I sure will!"

The car roared away. The man's crazy, Elmer decided. No telling what he might do if he found them. What had Jo brought down on them?

He went a short distance into the swamp and spread the tarpaulin under a canopy of vines and trees. He sprayed insect repellent on Spice and sat beside her. "We might have to rough it for a while," he said. "But, we'll manage, won't we?"

"Yep. I'm thirsty."

He handed her the canteen. "You sleepy?"

"A little, I guess."

Elmer stayed awake, listening. One could never know what a man like Smith might do. He could have sent Jo roaring off in the car while he silently searched them out. At the approach of dawn, he awoke Spice. "Be quiet now."

Elmer handed her a cup of pork and beans. "Better eat up. It's going to be a long day."

"I don't like them things."

"It'll be awhile before we stop and eat again."

She ate a small portion. "I'd rather have eggs and bacon, Poppy."

"Me, too."

He gathered their belongings. "We're going into the thick woods now. Just stay close behind me."

"I will, Poppy."

It took an hour to go a hundred yards. He felt relieved when they emerged from the thick undergrowth. He paused to rest. He carried everything wrapped in the tarpaulin hung over his shoulder. It weighed a ton. He wiped a sleeve across his face.

"It should be easy going for a while now," he told the girl.

"I'm glad. I don't like bushes."

"We'd better get moving," he said, loading up.

Deeper into the swamp they traveled. He was pleased now that the summer had been dry. Normally, the area they crossed would be knee-deep in water. He paused, waiting for a large cottonmouth snake to crawl out of their way.

"Shoot him, Poppy!"

"Can't risk that. Smith might be hunting us."

"He can see our tracks in the mud, Poppy."

Elmer stooped, passing under tangles of thorny bamboo vines.

The old man carried Spice across a shallow stream and went back for the pack. The heat became stifling. When he crossed the dark rivulet, he sat on the ground to rest. In the distance a shotgun blasted.

"What was that, Poppy?"

"My guess would be Smith. No doubt he came upon a snake. If he shoots everyone he sees, he'll soon be out of shells."

He knew he had to hurry. They crossed a knoll. In the fifties when deer were scarce in Georgia, he'd often hunted in the swamp. It was about the only place deer could be found. On the small hill he surveyed his predicament, wondering if Smith remembered Miss Mollie.

Elmer headed down the rise, turning west. Here, he followed a deer trail. They left no footprints on the packed trail.

In mid-afternoon they reached what was known as Snake Island. One had to be careful where he stepped.

"I'm tired, Poppy."

He stopped. Mud covered her overalls and boots. She sat on the ground and took off her straw hat. A bamboo briar had snagged a hole in the brim.

"How about some peaches?"

"Give me a lot."

He looked around for a place to camp. "It gets dark quick in the swamp. I think we'll hold up here for the night."

"Is that man still after us?"

"Hard to say, honey. He might have given us up and turned back. Or, might still be trailing us."

"What are you going to do, Poppy?"

"Wait him out. It's all we can do."

"We're going to stay in here forever?"

"No, don't you worry. We won't be here long."

The swamp's night life came alive in a crescendo of sounds. An owl led the chorus. Coyotes howled like screaming puppies. Crickets played the background. An alligator on the other side of the island snorted and splashed. Spice moved against him. A black bear tramped through the thicket not far away. Overhead, the moon slipped through a patch of clouds.

"You're supposed to make a fire, Poppy."

He wished he knew where Smith was. "Yeah, a small fire will add some cheer to this place."

"Build a big one, then. We need a lot of cheer."

Risking a small flame, he added twigs to keep it going. He listened for any sound that might betray the approach of a man or a dangerous animal.

He opened a can of pork and beans. Spice ate without arguing the menu. He offered her a small can of fruit cocktail. She devoured the fruit. "Care for a cookie?"

"I didn't know you brought cookies."

"I stuck in a pack for you."

A bear growled farther down the island. "It sounds mean, Poppy."

"Well, if he comes around here, I'll teach him what mean is."

Spice laughed nervously. "You'll shoot him, huh, Poppy?"

"If he tries to bother us, I sure will."

Elmer considered their plight. Had it been foolish to venture into the swamp at his age?. Every bone in his body ached and, every muscle pained. He almost fell asleep filling his pipe but forced himself to remain alert. Smith wasn't the only hazard. There were the packs of wild dogs.

"I'm scared, Poppy."

An owl screeched nearby. He threw a larger stick on the fire. "Nothing to be afraid of, honey." He patted the rifle he held. "You just remember that before anything can get to you it has to come through me."

She hugged his knee.

A cougar screamed.

"What in hell was that, Poppy?"

"Where do you learn such language?"

"They say it on TV all the time."

"I don't want you saying it, understand?"

"Yep. What was that making that noise?"

"A big cat."

"Oh, my God!"

He put an arm around her. "I see we have to have a long discussion about your TV watching, young lady."

Eyes sparkled from the fringes of the firelight. He cocked the rifle, waiting.

"That must be the devil, huh, Poppy?" She held tightly to his leg.

"More'n likely a wild dog. You sit still now."

A deep growl flowed from the pair of eyes. Elmer wished he'd brought his shotgun. He picked up a burning stick, holding it high. Another pair of fiery eyes reflected. The growls came louder. "I'm going to shoot that big one," he whispered. "You just sit still."

He aimed the rifle, squeezing the trigger. The bullet tore through the animal's chest. He withered on the ground, the high-pitched howl shutting the swamp into silence. The smaller dog ran off.

Spice drew a deep breath. Elmer wiped a hand over his forehead. "If Smith is out there, he'll know where we are now."

The cougar announced his location.

"Poppy?"

"Don't fret. He'll keep his distance."

"But how far is that?"

"Far enough that we don't have to worry about him."

"I sure don't like this place."

After a while, sleep overtook her. Elmer added more wood to the fire. At midnight, he could no longer hold his eyes open. He placed bigger wood on the fire and lay down next to Spice.

He jerked awake. Narrow slits of light streaked through the dense overhead to the dew-covered swamp floor. He listened, cradling the rifle. He thought he heard a twig snap. Elmer shook Spice awake. "We have to hurry."

He led the way deeper into the foliage. Coming onto a stream, he tested the depth. The water came up to his knees. Worried about quicksand, he searched for solid footing as he crossed. Depositing the pack, he returned for Spice and carried her over.

He paused to rest.

Toward noon, he found the old site for which he was looking for. Cautiously, he fought his way through an alley of overhanging growth. "Keep in my footsteps," he warned Spice. "There's an old well somewhere around here."

"What does an old well look like?"

"A hole in the ground."

"What is that?" she asked as they entered a small clearing.

"An old whiskey still."

She was too tired to question him further. He searched the ground up ahead.

He almost stepped into the hole before he saw it. Kudzu vines had grown up to hide almost completely the well. He held Spice's hand, leading her around the pit.

In the late afternoon, they emerged from the swamp into a clearing. A house with its tin roof rusting with age and its weathered boards bleached by years of sun and rain sat between two old chinaberry trees, their limbs twisted and broken.

The woman, thin and stooped, shoved wood under a black pot at the back of the house. She watched their approach from under the bib of a faded blue bonnet.

Shielding her face from the curls of white smoke, she stirred the clothes in the pot with a stick. As they neared, she wiped her hands on an apron, peering at them over small, steel-rimmed glasses.

Recognition signaled on her narrow face. "Why, Elmer, it sure has been a spell. Why ya'll coming out of them swamps?"

"How you, Miss Mollie?"

"Same as always, aging along with ugly. Bring that pretty little gal around to the front porch, and I'll fetch out some refreshments." Her dark eyes studied down on Spice who thought the woman must have been a thousand years old. The little girl had never seen such a long nose on anyone, nor a face so wrinkled.

Mollie brought glasses and a pitcher of tea to the porch. A large, red dog looked up from his snooze under a chinaberry tree. He sighed and returned to his only pastime.

"Elmer, what on earth ails ye, dragging that child through a jungle? What ye aim to do?"

He explained. "I was hoping you'd keep Spice here a day or two."

"Be glad to. Got a room in the attic where she can hide if anybody pokes around."

"They might. You remember Gus Smith?"

"That trash! Figured the law'd kilt him by now. I got my shotgun if he's up to testing me."

"You're old," Spice said.

Mollie laughed. "I be nearing ninety, young'un. That's sure enough old, ain't it?"

Spice giggled, stuffing down a peanut butter sandwich.

"Good young'un," stated Mollie.

She fed them supper; when it was dark, Elmer picked up his rifle.

"Ye isn't hoping to venture back into that swamp at night, are ye, Elmer?" She followed him out onto the porch.

"Not until in the morning. I'll just sit out here a while in case anyone comes prowling around."

"Ye be careful in there. He'll kill ye if he can. Lordy, who'd ever know? The animals would pick your bones clean afore the sun set!"

Chapter 7

Gus Smith had trapped, hunted, and fished the deep swamp during his teen years and probably knew his way around the dense woods better than anyone else. At least, he did when he lived at the edge of the marsh. Now, he wasn't so sure. Everything had changed. Water was where he did not remember it being. Dry land appeared where there should be water. Streams had filled or had been diverted in other directions by beaver or high water. Still, he thought he recognized Snake Island but couldn't be sure.

Gus had grown to be the largest of three boys. Standing six feet and four inches, he enjoyed shouldering his way through life. Weighing some solid two hundred and thirty pounds, he was seldom easy to intimidate, as a number of inmates had learned the hard way.

He considered himself a lady's man, and in fact, he was thought attractive by many women, including Jo Goodhand. A dimple in a firm chin and light wavy hair did make him stand out in a crowd. Deep blue eyes, penetrating when anger overtook him, led to some women aggravating him just to enjoy the results. Gus used women. He used Jo, and he wanted to use her daughter.

The old man was presenting a problem. If necessary, he'd kill him. Elmer Goodhand wouldn't be the first to be permanently consigned to the bogs. Gus remembered that a revenue agent had disappeared in the swamp while searching for a still. He always wondered if his daddy had anything to do with that. They never did find the agent's remains, not so much as a piece of clothing. The bog was an easy place to dispose of a body.

Gus paused, looking around. Something was wrong. He didn't remember there being big cedar trees in this section of the swamp. He must have turned the wrong direction back at the creek.

He'd made some connections in prison. He could get a continuing supply of cocaine and heroin in Miami, and he had contacts in Atlanta and D.C. who could handle everything he hauled out of Florida. He needed Jo's daughter. Cops seldom bothered a traveling family.

Gus cursed. An old man was sidetracking his plans. He wondered if Jo were in Goodhand's will. Probably not. It was more than likely the old man was leaving everything to his granddaughter. He certainly wouldn't be stupid enough to leave it to Jo, seeing as how she'd dumped the kid on him and skipped.

Who cared? That was peanuts compared to the fortune he stood to make. He wouldn't get caught this time. No more taking chances with the cops. He'd watch himself and only move the stuff on the weekends. Wasn't that when most families traveled?

He found his way out of the swamp just as night fell. He turned the car around and drove to the house.

Jo sat on the porch drinking a beer. She lit a cigarette as he sat in the rocker beside her. "Your old man's crazy," he said.

"We don't need the kid, Gus," Jo said.

"That's where you're wrong. I almost caught up with the old fool. Can't see how he traveled so fast with the kid along!"

"Remember, you promised not to hurt him."

"I told you I wouldn't, didn't I?"

"Why don't we drive up to Atlanta for the weekend? We can try for the kid next week."

"I ain't leaving until we get the girl."

"Do you think it's safe having the stuff in the car?"

"Naw, it ain't safe. It ain't never safe hauling dope, but what other choices do we have? You sure can't mail it."

"We could hide it here--maybe out in a barn. No one would ever think of searching here for coke."

"I don't know. I'll think about it."

"Gus, if they search the car-- "

"That's why we need the kid. The chances of getting stopped are slim if we've got her along."

"I don't like the idea, Gus. I never did, you know that."

"Hey, baby! We agreed, remember? We make a few hauls and dump her back here on the old man. Nothing to it. We'll be rolling in money. We'll take a trip. Go any place you want."

"I'd like to go back to California."

"Yeah, that's the place, all right. Any beer left?"

"I put a couple of cans in the fridge."

"Get me one, will you?"

She returned with the beer. "Sure dead out here," he said. "Don't know how I stood this country as long as I did. Ain't nothing to do but listen to the frogs and bugs."

"I hate it, too," said Jo. "Always did. Even when I was a kid. Never see anybody except the mailman."

Finishing the beer, he stood. "Tell you what. Let's stash the stuff in the barn and head up to Macon. Might find something to do there."

"There's more going on in Atlanta."

"And it's a devil of a drive, too. No, I don't want to fight I-75 unless there's some profit in it."

"Then I'd just as soon hang around here. Macon is a dead town."

"Suit yourself. I can stand this drag for a few more days, and then I'm pulling out."

"What about my kid?"

"We'll have her; don't you worry. One old man ain't going to upset our plans."

"Just remember your promise."

"Will you shut up about that?"

Jo lit a fresh cigarette. "Hadn't you better make that call?"

"Yeah, I'd better." He went inside. Later, when he returned to the porch, he cursed. "The delivery date has been set up. We're going to have to get the kid in the next day or two or make the delivery without her."

"In Atlanta or D.C.?"

"He wouldn't say. Said he'd give me the details in Atlanta. I told him I'd risk the Atlanta trip, but I'd have to have more money to make the run to D.C. without the kid along."

"I wouldn't make too big of a demand on them, Gus. You know how they can get when you do."

"Hey, they ain't dealing with no new kid, baby. I know what the market will bear. If they want the stuff hauled to D.C., they can do it. I ain't. Not for the Atlanta rate."

"Are you sure?"

"Hey, I'm sure."

Jo drew on the cigarette. "I'd like for us to get out of this business, Gus. It's too dangerous."

"We will once we've made enough money. Where else can you make ten grand for a couple of day's work?"

"But the risks."

"Relax. Nothing's going to go wrong. We'll just play it close to the chest and everything will turn out fine, and we'll be in some real money."

She relaxed. Gus always knew what he was doing. She finished the beer.

"Can you handle your kid, Jo?"

"What do you mean?"

"I mean we can't afford to have a trouble-making brat on these trips. Will she mind you?"

"I'll be able to control her."

"You'd better."

"Don't you go threatening her, Gus. I mean it."

"Sure. You just be sure you can handle her. There's too much at risk to have a brat drawing attention to us."

She looked across the moon-lit fields. "I don't even know her," she said quietly.

"Ain't that the way you wanted it? Didn't you dump her on your old man and take off?"

"Yeah. I did just that."

"Then stop worrying about it. What's done is done."

She studied him. "You never cared much about anything or anybody, did you, Gus?"

"Hey, I care about you, you know."

"Sometimes I wonder."

"You're not starting on that again, are you?"

She remained silent, lighting a cigarette. "Poor kid, out there in the swamp. We shouldn't have come here."

"Don't go soft on me, Jo."

"I'm not. I'll do my part. You just be sure we don't price ourselves into a lot of trouble."

"You worry too much."

"Prison has that effect on me."

"You want out?"

"You know what I want."

"Yeah. The good life. Easy money and good times. I know all about you, Jo."

"You don't know as much as you think. I don't want my kid or my dad hurt, but I know you when you get mad. You're liable to do anything."

"I done told you I wasn't going to hurt them, didn't I?" he said irritably.

"I know that's what you said."

"I gave you my word, didn't I? What's the matter with you?"

"You gave me your word about that woman, too."

He jumped up. "I thought you weren't going to throw that up to me again!"

He sat back down, brooding. "After all I've done for you," he mumbled.

She remained silent.

He lit a cigarette, drawing deeply. Suddenly, he clapped his hands. "Hey! I know where your old man gave me the slip. Yes, sir!"

"What are you talking about?"

"Remember that old woman -- what's her name?"

"What old woman?"

"The one who lives on the edge of the swamp by the old bridge."

"Miss Mollie?"

"Yeah, that's her name. That's where he took the kid as sure as I'm sitting here."

"Are you sure?"

"That's where he went all right. I'd forgotten all about that old woman. If she's still alive, that's where they are, and she's alive, I'll bet. You couldn't kill the old hag."

"If he left the kid there, we could get her easily enough," said Jo.

"I'll get her," said Gus. "First thing in the morning, I'll drive over there and get her."

"I'll go with you."

"No. You stay here in case Atlanta calls."

"And if my dad refuses to hand her over?"

"Hey. He's an old man. How much refusing can he do?"

"Plenty, when he makes up his mind."

Gus chuckled.

Chapter 8

Elmer Goodhand awoke with a start, his body wet with sweat. The darkness of the room crowded thick about him. On the nearby pallet, Spice turned over. A mosquito buzzed through the humidity. A small fan droned in the adjoining bedroom. Miss Mollie had permitted herself to use "high-priced lectric juice". She snored loudly.

He scratched a mosquito bite. Striking a match, he looked at his watch. Outside, the first hint of dawn urged a rooster to work.

Stiff and unsteady, Elmer got to his feet. Limping out to the back porch, he rinsed his face in a pan of water. The rooster crowed several times as if to warn that the day was going to be another scorcher.

Over the swamp a blue mist hung in streaks, pinching the tree tops from visibility. Inside, Miss Mollie began to stir, turning on a light. She appeared on the porch, pulling on her bonnet. " 'Tis another hot one, it 'tis. Why ye up so early, anyhow?"

"I been thinking, Miss Mollie. Smith might eventually put two and two together. Spice and I will leave as soon as there's enough light. I don't want to bring trouble on you."

"Git on."

"If he comes around, tell him we were here, but we left."

"I ain't telling him nothing. I'll fix ye and the young'un a bite. Likely be raining this morning, ye know."

"How can you tell?"

"My old rooster slept late for one thing. Another is the way the fog's clinging to them tree tops."

Miss Mollie's prediction came to pass as Elmer and Spice entered the swamp. A fine mist fell. "We're going to get wet, Poppy."

"Looks like."

"Where we going today?"

"Closer to home."

They stopped to rest near the well. Spice stood back from the hole. "Is it deep, Poppy?"

"About thirty feet as I remember." He threw a stick in the hole. It was awhile before he heard the splash.

"Let's go, Poppy. You might fall in."

The mist turned into rain. They moved through the kudzu tunnel and stopped under a large oak. Unrolling the tarp over bushes, he made their shelter under the spreading limbs.

While Spice changed into dry clothes, he stoked his pipe. She studied him, her arms thrust inside the bib of the overalls. "Poppy, when are we going home?"

"That's where we're headed, honey."

"Suppose that man is there?"

"We'll cross that bridge when we get to it."

"There's no bridge at our house, Poppy."

"A trouble bridge."

"I don't like trouble bridges." She frowned. "What's a trouble bridge?"

He explained.

"Well, shoot, Poppy, just cross it like you do other bridges."

"And how you do that?"

"Drive over it."

He chuckled. "We just might do that."

"I'm smart, ain't I?"

"Aren't I," he corrected.

"Sometimes you are."

The rain stopped. He took down the tarp, and they plodded deeper into the swamp.

"Hey, old man," Gus Smith's voice called from a distance behind them. "If you don't come out, I'm going to make you regret it, you hear? I'll get you today, and I'll leave your hide for the varmints!" He threw curses after the threats.

They hurried on.

Elmer avoided Snake Island, turning north through the bog, hoping he remembered where the old trail led. This was treacherous country, but he'd passed this way a few times years back on hunts. Nothing in the bogs remained constant. The land changed. He looked for an animal trail. It was awhile before he stumbled onto one. Swinging Spice up into his arm and watching for snakes, he picked his way through the grass as if walking on shattered glass.

Going only a short distance, he had to put her down and rest. Elmer wiped his face and fanned with his hat. He'd have to watch himself. It was easy to become overheated. He held the canteen for Spice to drink water and then drank some himself.

He carried her another short distance and rested. In places, the ground shifted under his weight. The swamp grass, their long blades stiff and sharp, pricked blood from his legs.

They made another trek, rested, and moved on through some of the most unstable footing he'd found. Still, he was on the animal trail and believed the ground would hold them. That was what he hoped--

He saw three dangerous snakes but knew there were many he didn't see. A moccasin was afraid of nothing. He'd give way to neither man nor beast, except as it pleased him to do so. Under normal circumstances, he would have shot a large cottonmouth that lifted his head high in the path ahead and dared him to approach. He wouldn't shoot now. Smith would be able to place their location by the sound of his rifle.

He waited. The snake eventually lowered his head and eased off into the tall grass.

Stringy moss hung from the stubby limbs of dead trees. The heat became stifling, making breathing difficult. It felt as if the air had died.

The trail led around a wide pool of stagnating, foul-smelling water. An alligator, twelve feet in length, lay like a bloated serpent on the other bank. Turtles sunned in bunches on fallen tree trunks sticking out of the water.

Overhead, crows cawed. A buzzard glided upward, easily riding a warped heat wave. The crows continued to argue loudly.

He rested, breathing hard. Dizziness surged over him. He wiped his eyes. Before the suffocating noonday heat swept in, he had to get out of the bogs. He'd never felt such mugginess.

In this place even the birds panted.

Elmer could see the end of the tall grass and lifted Spice. Slowly, panting, he reached solid ground. Putting her down and making it to the thin shade of a cypress, he dropped to the ground, gulping for air and sipping water.

Slowly, his vision blurred. The trees became silhouettes of shifting gray shades. He wondered if he should fire the rifle--three shots--to give Smith their location. What if he passed out--or died? What would happen to Spice? He pointed the rifle skyward to pull the trigger when his vision began to clear. He waited, dragging breath.

After a while, he felt better but allowed a few more minutes for his strength to return. Standing, his legs trembled.

"Poppy, you didn't look too good."

"I'm fine now."

She followed him into a gap through the undergrowth. A breeze found them on the other side, and he stopped to let nature fan them. He felt some better when they fought through another patch of thick undergrowth.

Under the shelter of a towering magnolia tree at the top of a knoll, he checked his directions. Satisfied, he sat down and opened a small can of beans and franks for Spice.

"You'll like these, honey. But we must hurry."

He opened a can of sardines for himself. "What is that?" she said, catching a whiff and looking closely at the contents.

"Little fish."

"They stink!"

"Won't argue that."

"Poppy, you don't have to eat them things. You can have half of my beans."

"I like sardines."

"Yuk!"

He watched her eat, unsure if anything he did anymore was right. What if he had died back there, or even now, for that matter? What would happen to her?

If he had given her over to foster parents earlier, none of this would have been necessary. That was something he'd have to keep in mind.

"Poppy, I'm still hungry."

He reached into the pack and brought out cookies. She smiled.

A shotgun blasted over in the bog. "He's canny, that one. Knew right where to pick up our trail. Well, one thing is for sure. He doesn't argue with snakes. I hope it was that mean moccasin he blasted."

"Maybe that big alligator will eat him, Poppy."

"That alligator doesn't want to tangle with that fellow. Smith poached bigger ones back when he was just a kid. Even wrestled them, I heard."

He knew they must hurry. As the afternoon settled and the shadows stretched, he reached his destination, an old logging road now mostly regrown, leading up beyond his pond. Where the road crossed a narrow stream, he lifted Spice and stepped into the water. Careful not to overexert himself, he followed downstream, stooping to pass under low-hanging branches and vines. He plodded on, his body aching and his leg almost numb.

Leaving the stream, he took care not to leave any tracks. Putting Spice down, he led the way into the thick undergrowth behind the pond dam. Clearing a small area, he unrolled the tarp and they sat down. Darkness slipped in.

"Poppy, we're nearly home!"

"Sure are. As a matter of fact, you can see the top of the house from up there on the dam."

She gave him a tired smile. "You're a top soldier," he said.

"Is that good?"

He nodded. "The best."

She grinned. "I stay with my poppy."

He pulled her close to him.

What now, old man? What do you do now? You can't go to the house. You can't start up the truck and leave because you don't know if Smith is behind you, closing in, or already at the house. You do know that he might kill you, so what now? How long do you plan on running? If you go to the sheriff, what will happen to Jo? She'd go back to prison, wouldn't she? So where do you go? You could always turn Spice over to them and be rid of the whole problem.

The hell I will!

Do you stay hidden in this jungle?

Let him come on. You'd be justified in killing him.

Yeah, you could kill the scoundrel.

They ate the last of their food and drank the last of the water.

He wondered how long Smith and Jo planned to stay at the house. He had to get closer and be where he could watch the house and their movements. A plan began to form in his mind.

Spice fell asleep, her head resting on his leg. The mosquitoes swarmed in, and he sprayed her with the last of the insect repellent. He gently moved her head from his cramped leg and pushed tobacco in his pipe. Elmer cupped the match to cover the light.

He let his mind dwell on his plan.

No, that wouldn't work. Yes, that might, but it would be too risky. Jo might get hurt.

He decided, for Jo's sake, that the best thing he could do would be to stay hidden. Maybe Smith would just leave and do whatever it was they planned to do. Puffing on the pipe, he swatted mosquitoes. Crickets and frogs made it impossible to hear if anyone approached. His imagination filled his ears with strange sounds. Twigs snapped. A disturbed limb swung back into position.

He was too old for such as this. Coyotes suddenly burst out with their screeching yelps, howling to the top of their lungs. Wild dogs hunted in a pack way back at the river. He waited for the moon to rise. There had to be a better way, and he thought he'd found it.

The darkness was total. He could not see his hand before his face. Fortunately, Spice was asleep. His own tired body sought sleep, but he forced himself to stay awake.

The moon, a bright ball of orange, spread sprinkles of light through the branches as it came up. The frogs belched in unison at the pond. Crickets scraped a racket. He shook Spice. It took awhile to bring her fully awake.

"Poppy, you know something?"

"What?"

"You're not supposed to wake little people up when they're asleep."

"Wouldn't you like to get out of these woods?"

"I sure would. There's mosquitoes bizzing everywhere."

"Then let's gather our stuff."

"What are you going to do?"

"I've got a plan."

Chapter 9

Elmer circled the house, hurrying along the edge of the cotton field. He approached a barn from the rear. A light shone dimly through the window of his study. It angered him that someone had trespassed on his private world. He saw Gus Smith's form by the upstairs window. Well, he at least knew Smith's whereabouts now.

The tobacco packhouse, a building once used for grading and tying cured tobacco leaves in bundles for the market, was a framed two-story barn having a cellar. Tobacco was usually placed in the cellar after being taken from the curing barn to remove the dryness. The pony's feed and tack were now kept in the packhouse.

Access to the cellar was gained through a trap door in the main floor. Back when the packhouse was used, the clay floor and walls were sprinkled with water to create the moisture necessary to render the tobacco leaves pliable.

The trap door lay hidden underneath scattered burlap bags. He found the lantern hanging just inside the door. By the moonlight slipping through the cracks of the wide door, he found the handle and pulled the trap door open. The rusty hinges yelled a long squeak.

He felt his way down the ladder among spider webs. Spice waited above. He struck a match and lit the lantern, turning it down low.

The poles once used to support sticks of golden leaves lay askew. Cobwebs hung from the walls, corners, and poles in threads of reflecting light. A heavy, dank odor filled his nostrils. It was like a step into the past. How many years had it been since he'd stepped down into this world of a bygone day? The floor and walls, once shining red clay, had faded with time. Dampness prevailed in the cool atmosphere.

Satisfied, he turned down the lantern and climbed out, gently closing the door and covering it with burlap bags.

"This will be a good place to hide," he told Spice.

"Poppy, I don't think I'd like to go down there."

"We may have to go down. There's nothing to be afraid of, you know."

"You didn't see all those spiders?"

"You mean spider webs."

"Poppy, there's spiders down there 'cause nothing else knows how to build webs; don't you know that?"

"They're old webs."

"I bet there's plenty of old spiders down there, too."

He broke a bale of hay and made Spice a bed, covering the hay with a saddle blanket. "There. You've got a soft place to sleep."

She stretched out on the blanket. "It's not as soft as my bed in my room."

"But it'll do for now, won't it?"

"Yep."

He watched the house through a crack in the door. "As soon as they settle down for the night, I'm going to slip into the kitchen and get something for us to drink and eat."

"You'd better be careful, Poppy."

"I will. Now should you wake up and I'm not here, that's where I'll be. I want you to stay here and keep quiet, understand?"

"By myself?"

"No. Spotty is right there under the shed. You won't be alone."

"Well, okay."

"Remember, you can't make a sound."

"I won't. I'll be *ssshhh* quiet."

She rolled over on her bed. "Bring me some ice cream."

"If I can."

When the lights in the house went out, he waited a half hour and left the packhouse. Entering the kitchen through the back door, he quietly searched for the flashlight that was kept in the pantry. He placed food in a bag they could eat out of the can, filled the canteen, took two of the six cokes out of the refrigerator and a carton of vanilla ice cream from the freezer. He was in the process of leaving through the back door when a car turned in the driveway and pulled around to the back of the house. Elmer ducked into the pantry and closed the double doors as someone entered the kitchen. "Hey, Gus, I'm here!"

Through the crack between the doors, he saw a heavy-set man with a beard open the refrigerator and take out a Coke. He sat at the table, opened the can, and guzzled. Gus, wearing only trousers, entered the kitchen. "About time you showed."

"Just got back from Macon. Wife said you called. Didn't say it was an emergency, though."

"The old man gave us the slip. He took the kid into the swamp. I lost track of them."

Elmer studied the bearded face. It was familiar. He finally put a name to the man. He was Gus's brother, Al.

"Seems to me you could've found them," said Al, turning up the Coke.

"Well, I didn't. That old man knows them swamps better'n I ever did."

"What you gonna do now?"

"Well, Al, I ain't got it all figured out yet. Me and Jo have got to get the shipment to Atlanta tomorrow. Figured you might want to try your hand at finding the old man and the girl."

"I don't know, Gus. I don't think I want to get involved with your deals. I've been in prison, and I didn't like it, I tell you."

"I've got a sure thing going. Few risks."

"Sure. Hauling dope out of Miami up the Interstate is a lark."

Jo entered the room. She opened the refrigerator. "Who's drinking all the Cokes?"

"Just got this one," said Al.

"I ain't touched them," Gus said. "How many's in there?"

Jo looked around the room. "I guess I must have drunk them. I lose track of things when I'm upset."

Gus turned back to his brother. "Will you at least keep an eye on this place until we get back?"

"And if the old man shows up?"

"Hold him and the kid here."

Al looked at Gus and then to Jo. "What you planning on doing with the old man? If you take the kid, don't expect him to sit back and ignore it."

"You don't worry about him. Just hold him for me," Gus said. "We might just take him to D.C. with us, just to keep an eye on him until this deal goes through."

Jo glanced at the pantry.

Elmer held his breath.

"Can't. I'm scheduled to pick up a load of produce in Macon in the morning for a haul to Nashville. Besides, like I said, I'm not getting involved in this thing. The way you both plan to use that kid doesn't set too well with me. Jo, that's your young'un. Why you doing this?"

"What do you mean? It's not like we plan to hurt her or anything. We're just taking her on a trip."

"Some trip. What if this is a sting operation? You don't ever know when the Feds are setting you up."

"I know these boys," said Gus. "You think I got into this business yesterday?"

"I'm out of it," said Al. "I've got a good job, and I ain't about to risk prison on a gamble. I don't care how big the money is."

"What about Spark? Think he'd be interested?" Gus wanted to know.

"Spark? Yeah, he'd do it. He'd kill his mother, if the money were right."

"Can you set it up with him? Tell him there's a thousand in it for him."

"I'll give you his number. You'll have to do the dealing yourself."

The pantry felt like an oven. Elmer dared not take a deep breath. He hoped Spice wouldn't wake up.

"Where'd you stash the coke?" Gus asked Jo.

"In one of the barns?"

"Which one?"

"The one down near where they keep the pony. The packhouse, Dad calls it. Anyway, it's that old two-story building."

"Let's go get it. We have to leave early in the morning."

"I don't know, Gus. Won't it be risky having the stuff here in the house or in the car? I mean, what if the cops showed up?"

"Why would they come out here?"

"You said Miss Mollie threatened to call the sheriff. Suppose she did? You don't know how much Dad told her."

"She's right," said Al. "Why take chances when you don't have to?"

Gus shrugged. "Man, you two are a pair. All right; we'll load the stuff in the morning."

Elmer took a deep breath. Perspiration dripped down his arms. The ice cream had started to melt. His bad leg felt numb. Slowly, he shifted his weight. The floor creaked.

"I heard something," Gus said.

"This old house squeaks and grinds all the time," said Jo. "What did it sound like?"

"I heard it, too," said Al, standing. "Sounded like it came from down the hall."

Gus pulled a .38 revolver from his waistband. "Stay here," he said, leaving the kitchen.

He soon returned. "We're getting jumpy. Ain't nothing moving around here except the wind."

Elmer remained frozen.

Later, after Al had departed and the house was quiet, he left the pantry and tiptoed to the back door. He pushed open the screen and slipped out.

He awoke Spice. "Better eat this ice cream before it completely melts, honey."

He'd wait until they'd eaten before moving to one of the other buildings.

"We have to move to the big barn," he told her later.

"Why?"

"Because they will be coming here in the morning to get something and would see us."

"Okay."

Leaving the packhouse, Elmer led the way behind the tractor shed to a large barn. He tested the ladder. He couldn't remember the last time he'd been in the loft. Last year Bill House had stored hay bales up there, so the structure must be sound.

It was an ideal place to watch the house. So long as they remained quiet, they wouldn't be detected. He made space for them behind an enclosure of bales, and Spice spread the blanket. "It's hot up here, Poppy."

"It is, but we'll make the best of it, won't we?"

"Yep."

"I'm going down for the food and rifle. You stay put."

"I will, Poppy."

Whatever the solution, he had to find it himself. Calling in the law was out since Jo was as involved as Smith. Jo desperately needed help, but the answer was not another term in prison. He had to keep away from Smith. He believed the man wouldn't hesitate to kill.

Was he living a dream? How had it happened? Suddenly, his world was turned inside out. His daughter had turned cold and calculating where her own child was concerned. What had happened to her? Where was the sense of it all? The streets of cities like Atlanta and Washington, D.C., were battlefields of slaughter, greed, and despair, and his daughter was helping to fuel the flames.

It was the age of the damned.

The march of the damned.

Senseless killings.

All for money, drugs, more money and more drugs.

The damned marched on.

Decadence. A society within a society. Idleness. Laziness. Greed. Hate, envy, and a perpetuating ignorance.

The fabric of sensitivity had dissolved.

The threads of compassion were stripped to the last single cord.

A dark, evil void had fallen like a shooting star, making a ghetto of minds to shift in a sea of enmity.

All for a substitute: an ingredient of permanent disablement--and death.

An evil possessed the land. The compassion is gone. The sensitivity is gone. The damned march to oblivion in a living hell--and straight to hell.

"Poppy?"

"I'm here, honey."

"Hold me."

Chapter 10

Elmer watched from the loft as Jo and Gus Smith left the house and drove the red sports car down to the packhouse. They were not long in the building. Both emerged carrying suitcases. Spice watched them from a knothole nearby. Gus placed the two bags in the trunk and slammed the lid.

Going over to the gate of the small corral, he talked the pony closer. Spotty hesitated, ears cocked forward. Smith pulled the pistol from his waistband, aimed, and fired.

The pony fell, his hind legs kicking violently.

Spice stared at Elmer, her eyes filling and her mouth trembling. "Pop-py?"

He crawled to her, holding her tightly, her whole body trembling. "Poppy?"

"Why did you do that?" Jo shouted.

"To let the old man know I mean business. You got any complaints?"

"You killed her pony!"

"Yeah." Gus chuckled.

Elmer heard Jo curse him. Smith laughed as he got into the car. "Let's get to Atlanta."

The car roared down the driveway.

It was awhile before they left the loft. Elmer wouldn't let Spice go out to the corral. He carried her to the house. She had cried herself weak. He put her in the tub, bathed her, and dressed her in the striped overalls, all the while listening for the sound of a vehicle that might be turning into the driveway.

He wondered who Spark might be. He'd never heard the name. Had Gus called him? Was he coming to the house?

When Spice was dressed, he picked up the rifle, and they hurried to where he'd left the truck. It wouldn't start. Elmer lifted the hood. The distributor cap hung loose. Smith had removed the rotary. "Looks like we'll have to walk."

He hurried back to the house to use the telephone. He called Rastus Wolfe. "Can you drive out here and pick me up, Rastus?"

"I'll be right out."

Hanging up, he hid the rifle behind a shelf of books in his study, hurried to his bedroom, and took a chest from the closet shelf.

When Elmer was discharged from the army after the war, he kept the .45 automatic pistol that had been issued to him. He, in fact, had stolen it, but that was a minor technicality where he was concerned. He'd carried the weapon through three campaigns and felt it belonged more to him than it did to the Army.

Shoving in the loaded clip, he stuck the pistol under his belt. Hurrying downstairs, he packed some of Spice's clothes in a bag.

"Where we going, Poppy?"

"I thought I'd let you stay with some folks 'til that man leaves."

"I want to stay with my poppy."

He made no reply.

The lawyer arrived a few minutes later. He glanced at the pistol. "Where to?"

"Your office. I'll explain when we get there."

Elmer left Spice in the care of the secretary while he and Rastus went into the lawyer's office. Elmer briefed the lawyer on everything that had happened in the last few days.

"Okay," said Rastus. "I understand your situation and how your hands are tied so far as getting the authorities involved, but your life is in danger. Maybe even the little girl's."

"That's why I need to find a safe place for her to stay-- preferably someplace out of the county. Do you suppose that couple you contacted about her sometime ago would be interested in keeping her for a while?"

Rastus reached for the telephone. "I'll ask them."

When he hung the phone up, he lit a cigar. "She's getting in touch with her husband to discuss it. Said she'd call me right back. I'm curious, Elmer. How you figure to cope with this thing?"

"You mean Smith?"

"And your daughter."

"I have a plan. You don't want to know the details."

"Don't do anything foolish, Elmer."

"Don't plan on it."

"Whatever you have in mind for Smith will eventually affect your daughter; you know that, don't you? If he's charged with anything, he'll involve her if for no other reason than to get back at you."

"That's how I've got it figured, too."

The lawyer studied him through cigar smoke. "I wish I knew what's running through your mind."

"Concern for my granddaughter."

"You haven't changed your mind about placing her in a foster home?"

"No. I'm more convinced than ever that she would be better off in that situation. What if something happened to me? Who'd look after her?"

"Her mother has priority, Elmer."

"Her mother's not responsible."

"How are you going to prove that unless you bring in all the facts--facts that would likely send her back to prison?"

The phone rang. When the lawyer hung up, he shook his head. "She said they couldn't take Spice under the circumstances. Said it might present too many problems."

"Have you a car or truck I can borrow?"

Rastus handed him keys to his car. "Take the Lincoln. I'll use my wife's car. I'll send a mechanic out to get your truck going."

"Thanks, Rastus."

The lawyer stood. "I can't see any way out for you, Elmer, so long as you're trying to protect Jo. If it weren't for that, we could pack Smith off to a Federal Pen in a hurry."

"I'll work something out, Rastus. I have to make it work."

"Just you keep in mind what kind of a hood you're dealing with. One mistake is all you'll get."

"I'll see you later, Rastus."

"For goodness sakes! Can't you hide that pistol? You look like one of them over-the-hill mobsters with that thing in your belt!"

"Do you know anyone named Spark?"

"Yeah, had him as a client once. Redheaded fellow in his late twenties. Why?"

"He might have been hired by Smith to watch my house."

"Well, you watch him. I defended him on a child-molestation charge. Always regretted winning that case, too."

"Lawyers."

"Everyone is entitled to a fair trial, Elmer. That's what we're about."

Elmer grunted. "Thanks for the loan of your car. I'll get it back to you as soon as I can."

Rastus waved his hand. "Don't hurry about it. Maybe if I have the wife's, she'll stop running up to Macon and spending money."

"Where we going, Poppy?" Spice said when they drove off in the Lincoln.

"To see an old friend."

He pushed tobacco in the pipe. "I'll get you another pony," he said.

She shook her head. A tear rolled down her cheek. She moved over beside him. "There's not another Spotty in the whole world, Poppy."

He turned north on I-75. The girl beside him sniffled. He puffed the pipe. "Want to play the radio?"

She shook her head.

An hour later he reached the turnoff. He traveled east until coming to an abandoned motel and turned down the next road to the right. The dirt road led past open farmland and pastures. Black Angus cattle grazed the hilly greens. An overloaded, battered pulpwood truck with a flat blocked a portion of the narrow road. He eased around it.

He pulled in the drive to an old, unpainted farmhouse and tooted the horn.

A tall, slender man near Elmer's age stepped off the porch and walked over to the car, spitting tobacco juice to one side. He grinned. "How about this! You old sonofagun. Elmer, what you doing in these parts? And look at this car! You steal it or something?"

"Borrowed. Belongs to a friend."

"Spice, this is an old army buddy of mine. His name is Luke McAllister."

"Hello," said Spice, watching him spit. "What are you eating?"

"Tobacco. I'm chewing it, honey."

"Poppy smokes his."

"Ain't she a treasure, though," said Luke, patting Spice's head.

Elmer got out of the car. Luke saw the pistol in his waistband. He spat. "Seems like I remember that piece, Elmer."

"It's the same one."

"Uh, huh," said Luke.

"How tied up are you here, Luke?"

"I ain't. My son runs the place. I mostly piddle with my snakes. What's the trouble?"

"I got plenty. It's a long story."

"I got time. We'll take the little girl inside. My daughter-in-law is feeding her baby. She'll dish up some goodies for Spice here while I show you some of the prettiest cows and rattlers you'll ever see."

"How many acres you got here now, Luke?" Elmer asked, following his friend into the house.

"A thousand or better."

"When you going to fix up this old house?"

"Didn't know it needed fixing. It don't leak nowhere. Cool enough in the summer and fairly warm in the winter."

"He hugs a penny where the house is concerned," informed his daughter-in-law, shoving a spoon of squash into her baby's mouth. "All he ever thinks about is nursing cows and milking snakes."

Luke winked at Elmer. "Young girls don't have no respect for elders these days, Elmer."

They leaned against the gate, looking at the Black Angus and Herefords grazing near the pond. Elmer told Luke about his predicament.

"Looks like you could use some help, old buddy."

"That's why I'm here."

"I ain't as young as I used to be," said Luke. "But I figure it don't take all that much energy to handle a shotgun--if the need arises."

"I need someone to keep watch at the house while I do some things in the cellar."

His friend hadn't shaved in a couple of days. Gray stubble contrasted with the tanned, weather-roughened face. Deep-set dark eyes searched Elmer's. Their friendship had begun in a foxhole and had lasted throughout the years. Each man owed the other for having saved his life.

"I'll throw some things together and ride back with you, Elmer."

Elmer lit his pipe.

In a few minutes Luke appeared on the front porch where Spice and Elmer waited. He didn't look like the same man. He wore a black suit, a gray hat and shiny cowboy boots. He carried a pump twelve-gauge shotgun cradled over his arm. Elmer saw a nickel-plated, ivory-handle single action Colt .45 stuck in his waistband.

"Where in the world did you get that, Luke?"

"Remember how I always wanted me a 'Peacemaker' after I saw General Patton with one strapped on his hip?"

"I remember. That's all you talked about."

"Well, sir. Last year I was up at the gun show in Macon and saw this revolver, and I grabbed it. Cost me a thousand dollars. It's authentic. A real Colt. Brand new, too."

"How does it shoot?"

Luke spat off the side of the porch. "About like you'd suspect."

"Is that good or bad?"

Luke winked. Elmer wondered what Rastus Wolfe would say if he saw Luke.

"Are you a cowboy?" said Spice, looking up at him.

"Well, I've got a lot of cows, and I'm a boy. What do you think that makes me?"

Spice looked at the guns. "An outlaw."

"You know, Elmer. I like this little gal." He patted her head. Luke threw his bag in the back seat, placed the shotgun on the floor, and lifted Spice into the car. "Let's go see about your bad boys, Elmer."

Chapter 11

Like the packhouse, the house also had a cellar. Years ago, Elmer had sealed the doorway to what Lucy had called the "dungeon". Entrance to the cellar was at the end of a narrow hall leading from the kitchen. Elmer had merely tacked a sheet of plywood over the opening to the cellar, enclosed the small hallway, and used the space as a closet. He doubted if Jo even remembered that the house had a cellar since she was hardly Spice's age when he sealed the "dungeon".

Elmer carried coffee out onto the front porch where Luke sat with the shotgun across his lap. The morning dew caught the early morning's sunrays, sparkling as mocking birds serenaded the start of a new day.

"The car's still there," informed Luke.

The blue Chevy was parked a short ways down the road from the driveway. "That would be Spark," said Elmer. "He's probably already called Smith and advised him that we're here."

Luke sipped coffee. "For his sake, I hope he doesn't decide to come up here. The young'un still asleep?"

"Yeah. Yesterday was rough on her--seeing her pony killed."

Finishing his coffee, Elmer took out his pipe. Luke poked tobacco in his mouth and propped his foot on the porch railing. "You ought to mow your grass, Elmer, or get you some chickens to kill the stuff."

Elmer ignored the remark. He stood. "Yell, if you need me. I'd better get to work."

"You think it'll work? I mean, what if they decide to come here and spend a week or more? You and the young'un'll be stuck in that cellar like prisoners."

"There's another way out."

"Where? I ain't seen one."

"The reason you haven't seen it is because it's under the side porch there and behind a couple brick pillars."

"Better stock it with plenty of food, water, and blankets. You could be cooped up in there for a while."

He went inside and began work. Inside the closet, he installed concealed hinges on the plywood sheet covering the entrance to the cellar. He fixed the panel where it could be locked from the other side. After rearranging the shelves, there was no indication that the plywood door was anything but a solid wall. All he had to do was stoop under a shelf and push the door open.

Old spiderwebs hung everywhere. The wooden steps creaked as he went down. The dirt floor and walls were solid clay. Shelves lined one side of the ten by ten-foot cellar. Fruit and vegetable bins were arranged along the other walls. Elmer unsealed the small door opening under the porch to let in light and fresh air. After an hour, he had the place in fairly good order and began stocking it. From an electrical circuit in the closet, he ran a wire to the cellar and installed a receptacle.

"Should have done this years ago," he told himself. "Makes a good storm shelter."

He carried down a fan and small light. Remembering that someone had given Lucy a card table for her birthday some years back, he located it in the attic. He found other treasures there, too. When he was through, the cellar was furnished with two folding lawn chairs, a break-down army cot, a foam rubber mattress, pillows, and blankets.

"Are we going to live down here, Poppy?" Spice asked from top of the cellar stairs.

"It's our retreat," he said. "No more hiding out in the swamp or barn."

"There are no windows," she discovered, coming down the steps. "And where will I sleep?"

"Everything's taken care of. It'll be like camping."

"It'll be like staying in a hole in the ground, Poppy."

"But we'll be safe."

"It doesn't look too safe. What's all that hanging up there?"

"Dried-out onions, ears of corn, and do-dads."

"Is *that* what we're going to eat?"

He took her on a tour of the cellar, swore her to secrecy, and ushered her to the kitchen for breakfast. Luke came in to refill his coffee cup. "Where you been, Spice?"

"It's a secret, Mr. Luke."

"That's a girl."

Spice finished her breakfast and went into the den to watch a cartoon video. Elmer joined Luke on the porch.

"You really intend sticking it out down there if they come back here?"

"I intend to have a place to hide Spice."

"Let me take her home with me."

"I thought about that, but I have a feeling that if Smith found out, you and your family would be in great risk."

"My sitting here with a shotgun is not a risk?"

"Not like it would be if you had what they were looking for."

"How would they know?"

"I don't know that they would, but you never know where they have eyes and ears. Look at how law enforcement is infiltrated."

"Yeah. One of our deputy sheriffs was recently indicted," said Luke.

"My daughter is in over her head, Luke. She's in with a bad bunch. I've got to get her out."

"You won't. Not unless she wants out. What makes you think they'll hang around long enough for you to do anything?"

"They want Spice."

"Elmer, I don't see how you can do anything but hide."

"There's one thing I can do."

"What? You can't go to the law. All you can do is get yourself killed."

"Getting rid of Smith is the key," said Elmer, puffing on his pipe.

Luke spat off the porch. He wiped his mouth, studying Elmer. "How you going to do that short of killing him?"

"If he dies, it won't be at my hands."

"I don't want to hear about it," said Luke. "Knowing nothing is to testify about nothing."

He studied Elmer through squinted eyes. "Has it occurred to you that your daughter might be too involved to ever get out?"

"It has."

Luke moved the .45 Colt under his belt. "The quickest way out of this, where you and the young'un is concerned, is to call in the law."

"I'm aware of that, but how do you sacrifice your own child? I keep hoping for a change. Maybe, just maybe, there's a chance."

"Sometimes there ain't, Elmer."

"I know."

A black pickup truck pulled off the road behind the blue Chevy. A man got out. Spark left his car, and they stood talking between the vehicles.

"Wonder what that's about?" said Elmer.

"Us."

After a few minutes, Spark drove off, and the pickup remained. "We've got a new boy," said Luke. "This Smith character must have a network of sorts."

"Looks like it," said Elmer. He withdrew a piece of paper from his shirt pocket. "I found this in the bedroom where they stayed. It's a telephone number in Atlanta. I called it. It's a motel. I think it's where they went to make the dope delivery."

"Well, Elmer, all you have to do is wait for Smith to make a delivery without Jo along. You call the Federal boys, and they solve your problem."

Elmer shook his head. "If he's caught, he'll implicate Jo."

"There's two fellows in that truck down yonder," said Luke. "I just saw the other one."

"Maybe they're expecting Smith soon."

"Could be, so you'd better decide what you want to do."

"We stay put. When he sees us with all this artillery, he'll leave faster than he drove in."

"I like the sound of that," said Luke.

They waited.

The afternoon dragged on. He put Spice down for a nap, and they waited on the porch, drinking coffee and watching.

They were old men with a common background. Each had earned a Purple Heart and medals for this and that, none of which meant much now. Armed, they were prepared to fight another battle--one that they might lose. But then, they could have just as well lost all the other battles they had fought. If they had lost, the world would have been a different place. It is doubtful that drugs would have been a problem in that world. Slavery has a way of mastering incidental problems.

They wondered, sometimes, where the years had gone. This was the sunset, the evening. Darkness was around the corner. Life prolonged is death pending.

Inside the house was a little girl--a child caught between forces that would ensnare and strangle her. A mother addicted is no parent. She would sacrifice that which should have given her a reason for living.

They took turns at watch, one guarding while the other slept. It was like old times in a far-away foxhole.

The next morning Luke's daughter-in-law called to inform that her husband had an accident and broke his arm hitching equipment to a tractor.

"Sorry, Elmer. Looks like I'm going to have to get back."

Elmer drove him home.

Driving back to Action, he wished he could continue on to Florida with Spice but such was impossible. He had to see this thing through.

He waited until it was dark before driving past the farm.

The red sports car was parked in front of the house, so were Spark's car and the black pickup.

He drove to Mavis Hornberry's house out on the edge of town, but she wasn't home. He remembered that she was visiting her sister in Savannah.

"You know something, Poppy?"

"What, honey?"

"Bad people make life skippy, don't they?"

"That's a fact."

"Why don't we go eat?"

Driving to a fast-food establishment near the Interstate, he ordered a bucket of fried chicken and drove to the Wolfe residence.

Janet Wolfe sat them at the booth in the kitchen and poured tea. Spice selected a drumstick. Janet tucked a napkin in her collar. "I'm not getting a haircut," Spice said.

Later, the lawyer led Elmer into the den. "Elmer, I ran into a friend of mine this morning, and we did a little speculating. He's with the FBI. He and I go back aways. Went to law school together."

"You didn't mention any names, did you, Rastus?"

"Of course not. It was all hypothesis. In summary, it boils down to John Hypothetical being in a no-win situation with a lot of hazards."

"We already guessed that."

"The bottom line is that Action, Georgia, is fast becoming a hold-over point for a major narcotic's operation. My friend couldn't provide any specifics--only bits and pieces of information he'd picked up from the narcotics boys. Reading between the lines, I'd guess the Feds are keeping their eyes open where Action is concerned."

"Reckon they suspect Smith?"

"My guess is that they are watching him; if they are, that means they're looking at his companions, too. Actually, Elmer, I don't think you have much time to do whatever it is you plan to do to rescue your daughter."

"Looks that way."

"One more thing. If the Feds suspect Action is a hold-over point, they'll be looking for the place where the substance is stored. That means they could trail Smith right to your place. If they do, they'll wonder what kept you from advising the authorities."

"I appreciate your telling me all this."

"I'm going to give you some free advice, Elmer. Take your granddaughter and go someplace--preferably out of state--until this thing comes to a head. I can promise you I'll see to it that Smith's name gets put on the proper list."

"A list that will automatically include Jo's name."

Rastus shrugged. "Some things can't be avoided, Elmer."

"No, thanks, Rastus. I'll stick around."

"With a plan?"

"I'll do what I have to do."

"Well, whatever you do, don't go to the local authorities without first checking with me. There's some question concerning the integrity of a couple of them."

"Which ones?"

"That's the problem. I don't know."

"I saw my truck outside. We'll be leaving now. Thanks for the use of your car."

He drove by the house. The vehicles were gone. He continued down the road a mile, cut the lights, turned around, and drove back. Still seeing nothing, he turned in at the lane leading up by a corn field. He parked the truck in a growth of pines, and they walked toward the house.

Elmer turned a corner at the large barn before he saw Spark. The man held a pistol in his hand, though not pointed at him.

"Get up to the house," Spark demanded. "Gus is waiting for you two."

Chapter 12

"Well, old man," Gus Smith greeted. "You've been a pain. It's a good thing I'm in a good mood today. I'm going to forget about all the problems you've caused but only if you behave yourself and not give us any more trouble."

Spark pushed him down onto the sofa. Elmer looked over at Jo. "I'm sorry, Dad, but you did cause us a lot of delay." Spice stood on the couch beside him.

"Get the kid ready," Smith told Jo. "Be sure you pack enough of her clothes."

"Where you taking her?" Elmer demanded.

"None of your business!" snapped Smith.

"That wasn't necessary," Jo said. "He deserves to know." She sat on the couch. Spice tried to move closer to Elmer. "We're heading for Florida, Dad. We'll only be there a couple of days."

"Why don't you give him our schedule, Jo?" Smith said irritably. "I don't want everybody knowing my business!"

Smith walked over to the couch, standing over Elmer. "If you get any ideas, old man, you just remember your daughter's in as deep as me. And we'll have the kid."

"How long you plan on keeping her?"

"As long as it takes."

Elmer looked at Jo. She turned away.

"Poppy, I want to stay with you," Spice pleaded.

"We'll be back to see Poppy real soon," Jo told her.

"I'm staying with my poppy."

Elmer took her in his arms. "You go with them, honey. I'll see you soon. Don't cry now."

"Get her things." Smith told Jo. "We're running late as it is."

"What do I do with Pop here?" asked Spark when Jo left the room.

"He ain't gonna do nothing. He knows what'll happen to the kid if he does. You can take off after we leave."

They readied to go. Spark ushered Elmer out to the porch. Spice hugged his legs tightly. "Poppy?"

"I'll see you soon," he said. "You go along now and do what they tell you."

"You promise, Poppy? You promise I'll see you soon?" Her lips trembled.

"I promise."

Smith chuckled.

Elmer stood on the porch, watching their tail lights disappear down the road.

The house became a tomb. He wandered from room to room, his insides boiling. Why hadn't he been more careful? How had he been so stupid as to walk into their trap? He feared what Smith might do to save his own hide.

Elmer made a decision.

The next day he drove the truck to Action and bought a late model used car having dark tinted windows. He liked the quick response of the light blue Dodge. "I'll pick my truck up in a few days," he told the salesman.

He returned home, packed a suitcase, and changed into a creamed-colored suit. Shoving the .45 under his belt, he left the house.

The Dodge crept to ninety before he realized it, passing everything on I-75. He slowed to sixty. No need to hurry, he told himself. Watch yourself; it'll work out.

He found the motel on the north side of Atlanta. It was one of the newer ones. Some people were sunning themselves at the pool. The Poor Southern restaurant across the street appeared crowded. He checked into the motel, but he didn't unpack.

Elmer walked around the building, a two-story, three-winged affair having a colonial style, then crossed the street to the restaurant. After serving his plate at the salad bar, he sat at a table to observe the entrance to the motel, wondering just how much drug trafficking went on in such places. He knew little about the criminal mind but had always thought such things were done at seedy-looking places.

He didn't look for Smith to show up for several days, if at all. It was pure guessing on his part that they would make delivery at the motel where he'd called his contacts. Elmer was there because it was the only thing he knew to do.

It suddenly occurred to him that Smith's associates might have the motel staked out, looking for signs that would indicate the presence of police. Elmer was realizing the thing could get really complicated. He told himself he'd better watch his step and not do anything that would bring attention to himself.

Returning to his room when night came, he pulled on his coat, turned out the lights, and cracked the door, looking along the rows of cars parked in the lot. Leaving his room, he walked around the building, searching for a red sports car but doubting that he would find it.

Still, he made the rounds twice more before going to bed. It was a routine he would follow for a week.

He wondered if he should give it up. He had probably guessed wrong. Smith could have already met his contact elsewhere. Elmer decided to give it two more days.

He saw the red car on a rainy night. Having neither a raincoat nor an umbrella, he hurried to his car parked on the other side of the motel, getting soaked. Driving around to the back, he parked within sight of the red car. Later, when the rain slacked, Smith left a room on the second floor and hurried down to the car. Looking around, he unloaded two suitcases from the trunk and quickly returned to the room.

Elmer waited, hoping to see Spice.

An hour passed before the door opened. Jo followed Smith out of the room holding Spice by the hand. They walked across the street to the restaurant. He felt relieved to see the child appeared all right.

How to get her away from them?

Could he pull it off?

When they left Poor Southern and returned to their room, he was still deliberating how to safely get his granddaughter. He lit his pipe.

Near midnight three men stopped outside Smith's room. Looking around, they lightly tapped on the door, then quickly entered. Ten minutes later they left, two carrying suitcases.

What if Smith decided to leave now that the delivery was made? Would he have to approach the man with drawn pistol to get Spice?

Hurrying out of his car and over to the sports car, Elmer opened his pocketknife and stooped down. He ducked as the headlights of a vehicle turning into the lot swept by. The couple parked in the space five cars down. He stayed down while they unloaded the trunk, wondering if they would ever complete the task.

He was in the process of puncturing the right rear tire when Smith stepped out onto the balcony. Elmer lay flat on the pavement, close to the car.

Jo joined Smith, both lighting cigarettes. He heard Smith chuckle as he turned up a can of beer.

Throwing the empty can aside, Smith started down the stairway. Elmer rolled under the pickup parked in the next space. He could have reached out and touched his enemy's leg. The drug trafficker rummaged through the back seat of the car, then slammed the door shut, and went back upstairs. Jo and he returned to their room.

Were they planning to leave?

He thrust the knifepoint into the tire. Air hissed. Hurrying to the other side, he worked the knife quickly, cutting his hand in the process. As the air escaped, Elmer rushed to his car. Getting inside, he grabbed quick breaths. Examining the wound and relieved to see it wasn't serious, he wrapped his hand with a handkerchief. Blotches of blood spotted his trousers.

He waited another hour. Satisfied they were staying overnight, he drove around to the other side of the motel, washed his hand, and changed into dry clothes. The suit looked ruined.

Placing his suitcase in the Dodge, he drove back to where he could observe the red car and the room. It was eight in the morning when Smith discovered the two flat tires. He looked around. Elmer could see his mouth spouting profanity.

Smith hurried up the stairway. In a moment Jo and Spice appeared on the balcony. Smith returned to the car, reexamined the rear tires. He called Jo down. They appeared to be arguing. Elmer, remaining slumped down in the seat, heard Jo tell Spice to stay in the room, that they'd be back in a minute.

Elmer waited until they had entered the passageway through the building. He drove the car into a space down from Smith's car. He jumped out, leaving the motor running and ran up the stairway and knocked on the door. "It's Poppy, Spice," he called.

The door swung open. He grabbed her hand. "Hurry!"

Rushing down the steel steps, he tripped but caught himself. He shoved Spice in the car. "Get down on the floor," he said, sliding in.

Backing out of the space, Elmer drove slowly out of the parking lot. He saw Smith and Jo coming out of the office as he turned up the street.

He didn't let Spice get up off the floor until they were heading south on the Interstate.

She hugged him tightly. "We showed them, huh, Poppy?"

He felt good, despite his aches. "Did they hurt you or treat you mean?"

"He hit me," she said, pulling up her dress and showing him the bruise on her leg. "The woman spanked me, too."

"She's your mama, Spice."

"I don't want no mama. I got my poppy."

The old man grunted.

Leaving the downtown congestion, he looked for an exit that would lead them over back roads to Action. Three miles later, he turned off the Interstate, and only then did he relax. He pulled in at a service station for gas. He lit his pipe. "You want something to drink, Spice?"

"You know I do, Poppy."

Believing that Jo would be worried when she discovered Spice missing, he called the motel. Jo answered the phone, her voice hardly audible.

"I've got Spice, just in case you're worried about her."

"I am! I was nearly out of my mind."

He heard muffled sounds. Smith's voice boomed over the telephone. "Old man, I've had my fill of you. I'm fixing your case when we get back! You just jinxed a big deal for me."

Elmer hung up the telephone. His patience had also reached the limit. It was time to put an end to the nonsense, and he hoped he would be up to it.

"Poppy, I'm hungry. I haven't had any breakfast."

"We'll get something down the road."

"You know what?"

"What?"

"I'll be glad when we're home. I'm tired."

"We might have to hide in the cellar for a while. Can you do that?"

"Yep."

"I might have to leave you there alone now and then."

"Why?"

"To do some things."

"I can help you."

"I know you could, but I need you at the cellar to keep your ears open, to listen, and to tell me what's going on."

"Aw, that won't be no fun."

"I'll pay you."

"How much?"

"Oh, several dollars."

"Make it, uh, let me think." She looked up in deep thought. "How about a thousand dollars?"

"You could buy a whole gallon of ice cream with that much money."

"Don't you know nothing, Poppy? I could buy that many gallons." She held up ten fingers.

"I'll think about it. You're sure expensive."

"Are girls supposed to be expensive?"

"They usually are."

"That's fine. Expensive sounds nice. I think I'll buy me a pony with my money."

"I know where there's a real pretty one."

"You do? You're the best Poppy in the whole world. Did you know that?"

"Yes. You told me that before."

She stared out the window at horses grazing in a pasture. The rolling country looked drought-seized, crops wilted under a blazing sun. Spice curled up on the seat, her head resting on his leg. He glanced down at the tired youngster, wishing he were younger with reasonable assurance that he could live to see her grow up. There were few options where she was concerned to ensure some kind of future for her. It would be a tragedy for Jo to take custody of her. The child's life would be ruined.

Elmer remembered his grandparents. His father's parents had lived with them when he was a child. He sensed that they cared little for children. They believed that a child should be seen and not heard, that offspring were field hands, and that the sooner they were put to work, the better.

Chores took priority over school. When there was work to be done, the children should do it--even if it meant staying out of school. It was enough that parents brought them into the world. Let them earn their keep when they reached six years.

He could not remember them ever saying a kind word. Their ailments were of the utmost importance and underlined every conversation. Elmer wasn't too sad when they passed on. Strange that he should be thinking about that now. He really shouldn't blame his grandparents. They were probably treated the same way when they were children. He wondered if Spice would ever forgive him for what he had to do.

In Action, he left the Dodge at the car lot, drove the pickup home, and parked it in the woods behind the pond. They walked to the house. "Poppy, how come we have to stay in the cellar?"

"Because I have plans for Mr. Smith, and we have to be here to carry them out."

Chapter 13

Jo had never seen Gus so angry. He threw the ice bucket across the room. He cursed her, the vile profanity chilling her. "Gus, at least Spice is safe."

He slammed a fist to her face. "Shut up!"

Pain pounded through her ear. She fell on the bed, frightened.

"That old man has had it!"

She wiped away the tears.

"Imagine that old fool coming up here. How'd he know we'd be here?"

"I don't know. I didn't tell him."

He cursed again. "Nobody cuts my tires. Nobody!"

He sat on the edge of the bed. "We've got a good deal going, and your old man is fouling up the works."

Jo left the bed, going to stand near the window. Rain pelted the parking lot. When she discovered Spice missing, she'd nearly gone out of her mind, never feeling so helpless. She'd thought she had lost the ability to care about anything except Gus. At one time that would have been true. It wasn't anymore.

She turned to face him. "Gus, we don't really need the kid. How many more trips do you plan to make before we quit?"

"I ain't about to quit. Not yet. Not with the money we're raking in."

"You promised."

"I ain't promised nothing! I'm getting my share while the getting is good."

She wore light red slacks and a low-cut, black blouse. She tried to keep herself attractive to please Gus. Jo knew he liked showing her off to the people with whom he did business. It served his ego to have an attractive woman around.

She'd learned a lot about Gus in the past few weeks, seeing hidden traits that frightened her. He would never quit dealing in drugs. He liked the excitement and money too much. She sensed Gus feared the men he dealt with as much as she did. They had made it clear what would happen to him, and her, if either presented a problem--any problem.

"We're arranging for you to make a delivery to D.C.," the one named Brockton had told him. "You've proved up, so far."

Brockton appeared to be the leader of the group. The large man's smiles always appeared menacing. Two men who handled the money and the haul usually accompanied him. Jo had never heard either speak a word. All three carried automatic weapons.

"Traveling with a kid is a good idea," Brockton had told Gus. "The family image gives you an edge."

Jo believed Gus feared what Brockton might say if he found out that they no longer had Spice with them.

They went to dinner across the street. "We're pulling out in the morning," said Gus.

"I thought we were going to do some shopping on this trip."

"That can wait. I got things to do in Action. You heard what the man said."

He later apologized for hitting her.

"Forget it," Jo said, looking out the window.

Gus cut into his steak. "There's money to be made in this business. All we have to do is watch ourselves, and we'll be rich. Have anything we want."

She wasn't so sure and was beginning to think she'd made a mistake in picking up the old life but it was too late now to get out. Gus wouldn't let her, and it was clear that Brockton would not let Gus out so long as he was useful to him.

They arrived in Action in the middle of the afternoon and drove out to the farm. She saw no sign of life. The truck was gone, and she was glad. She had not expected her father to return to the house with Spice. She wondered where they had gone and hoped it wasn't anywhere close by. Gus had so many people--relatives and friends, keeping a lookout for them. Many of them would do anything for money or drugs.

The farm brought back so many memories. She couldn't exactly remember why she had disliked living there. All she knew was that she couldn't wait to get away. There was no excitement in the country. It was too quiet and isolated. Still, that wasn't a valid reason, looking back on it. Her dad had bought her a car during her last year in high school, and she did drive around a lot with her friends.

"Get me a beer," Gus demanded, sitting in one of the porch rockers.

Jo thought she heard something when she entered the kitchen. The noise sounded like it came from the closet near the kitchen. Probably mice, she thought, opening the door to look. Crediting it to her imagination, Jo closed the door and went out onto the porch.

"I'd sure like to know where your old man took the kid," said Gus. "If I had the time, I'd do some searching. He might have taken to the swamp again."

Jo swallowed a sip of beer and lit a cigarette. "You might never find them."

"I will. I got plenty of people watching. He can't hide forever."

"You don't know my father."

"I know him, and I'll find him, you'll see."

"Only if he wants you to."

"What's that supposed to mean?"

"Just that. My father's old, but he's no fool. It just might be he's as tired of you as you are of him."

"Never thought I'd hear you defending him."

"I'm defending no one. I'm just stating a fact."

"He's crazy."

"Yeah. Like a fox. Look how he went about getting Spice back."

"And you're glad."

Jo shrugged. "We can make the trips without her."

She knew Gus wasn't listening. He never listened to anyone. He had all the answers. Suddenly, she wanted to tell her father she was sorry, sorry for dumping Spice on him and for all that was happening. She never should have come back.

A car turned into the driveway. Spark and a man she recognized as Gus's cousin got out.

"Was hoping you'd be back," said the cousin.

"What's up?"

"Nothing. Not anything you can put your finger on," replied Jim Lee Smith, a small, thin man in his early thirties. His biggest ambition in life was to win a car race, any car race.

"So spill it," said Gus impatiently. Jim Lee spoke with a long, slow drawl.

"I told him there wasn't nothing to it," said Spark.

"Shut up, Spark," Gus ordered.

"Well, I know this woman, you know. We're chummy if you get my drift."

"Get on with it!" demanded Gus.

"Just rumors," said Spark.

"Will you be quiet?" Gus snapped.

"She said her girlfriend's boyfriend--he's sort of a part-time deputy sheriff--says there's some new faces going in and out of the sheriff's office as well as the police department. Said he suspected they was Feds."

Gus laughed. "So?"

"Well, Spark said you said to keep an eye on things."

"I didn't mean the cops, dummy!"

"Well, shoot, Gus, if there's Feds hanging around, you oughta know that, too."

"I do, but I ain't interested in third or fourth-hand information about someone visiting Action cops. You boys go and find Jo's dad and her kid. They're the ones I want."

"We'll find them," said Spark. "Hey, I thought y'all had the kid with you."

Gus explained.

"Well, can you beat that?" said Jim Lee. "Of all the nerve. Picked her up right under your nose, eh?"

Gus stared at him. "That's what I said, wasn't it?"

Jim Lee chuckled. "I could have told you that old man is nervy. I remember Pa saying--"

"Forget that!" barked Gus.

"Whatever you say," Jim Lee said.

Gus finished his beer and lit a long cigar. It was a new thing with him. He was beginning to like the taste. And there was a certain something about a moneyed man smoking a cigar. "You boys just stick to trying to spot the old man and the kid. You might want to keep an eye on this place, too. Jo and I are leaving in the morning for Florida."

"Shoot, he wouldn't be coming back here," said Jim Lee. "Not after stealing the young'un from you the way he did."

"He might," said Spark. "He does strange things."

"Well, I say--"

"Just keep an eye on the place," interrupted Gus. "That don't mean you have to park in the driveway. Make a couple rounds out here at night while we're gone. If you see him, don't do anything. All I want is to know where I can find him when I get back."

"I need a little cash," said Spark.

"Me, too," added Jim Lee.

Gus dug into his pocket, producing a roll. He handed each a hundred-dollar bill. "Stretch it out. I'm not made of money."

Jo went into the house to make a sandwich. She was thinking of Spice and wishing to see her. No, she didn't wish that or want to become attached to the kid. There were too many responsibilities connected with a child. What would she do with her when they started traveling? There were places to go and things to do, and a child didn't fit in with their plans.

She tried, with little success, to blot from her mind the possibility of what Gus would do if he found her father. She would remind him that nothing could be gained by harming him--nothing.

Gus wasn't mean. He just had a quick temper, and he was always sorry afterwards; wasn't he?

She would be glad when they left in the morning. She would have the trip to think about. Traveling always cleared her worries.

Jo hoped Spice wasn't hungry or anything.

Gus entered the kitchen. "They're good boys," he said. "They'll find them if anyone can."

"I didn't think Spark cared for the swamp."

"He don't no more. Not since he saw some hairy giant in there."

"Did he really?"

"Says he did. For sure, he ain't about to go back in there alone. Makes no difference. The old man's holding up someplace with friends, is my guess."

"Suppose he goes to the police?"

"He won't. Not when it would send you back to prison." He laughed.

Chapter 14

Voices from above the cellar came through the floor as muffled sounds. Some of the words Elmer could make out. Spice sat at the card table drawing. He was glad he'd remembered to bring down some of her dolls and coloring books. The small bulb of the night-light provided a soft glow in the dark room.

Waiting a half-hour after hearing the car leave the next morning, he cracked the door of the closet and listened. Hearing nothing, Elmer stepped into the kitchen and looked out. The red car was gone. He called Spice.

"Poppy, I like daylight better. I don't like being in a hole."

"The cellar's not too bad. We'll stick this thing out, won't we?"

"I guess. I done colored everything. I've even colored the colors."

"That's what artists do."

"I wouldn't want to be one of them."

He cooked eggs, grits and bacon, going to look out the front whenever he heard a car on the highway. From what he'd heard of their conversation, Smith and Jo would be on their way to Florida. When they were finished with breakfast, he returned everything as he had found it.

He heard a car slowing down on the road. He went to look out a window in the den. He recognized Spark's truck. A car approached from the other way and stopped beside the truck. Both vehicles now turned into the driveway. He rushed Spice through the closet. He remained at the top of the steps, his ear to the door.

He heard footsteps entering the kitchen. There were two of them. He didn't recognize the other's voice. "We'll search the house first," said Spark. "Make sure you leave everything like you found it. I don't want Gus getting suspicious."

"So what? He'll think it was the old man."

"Don't bet on it."

"I think we're wasting our time. Why would Gus stash his money out here?"

"Can you think of a better place? Do you think he'd be fool enough to put it in a bank?"

"How much money are we talking about, anyway?"

"Well," said Park. "Figure it for yourself. He delivers in volume--large quantities. He takes in a lot of dough for that kind of operation. Besides that, he delivers the payoff back to Florida. We ain't looking for peanuts."

"If he ever found out--"

"Yeah. He'd come after us like--"

"He'd suspect Goodhand."

"Can't be sure."

Elmer heard them searching through the rooms. The possibility that Gus was hiding money on his place had not occurred to him. But, why not? He hid drugs there.

An hour later, the two men left the house. Elmer opened the cellar's outside door a crack and peeked out. He saw Spark and the other man hurrying to the barn. Spark's companion wore a deputy's uniform.

The men made a hurried search of the outbuildings. Elmer watched as they returned empty-handed. He thought this was an interesting turn of events. Easy money attracted vultures of all sorts.

In the evening, Elmer and Spice went out onto the porch. A warm breeze stingily fanned a side porch. Elmer sat where he could view the drive. Spice rocked in the chair beside him. "You know something, Poppy?"

"What?"

"I'll be glad when it snows."

"It never snows this far south."

"It doesn't?"

"Never has, except for a few flakes during a freak weather condition."

"Where does it snow the best?"

"Up north. It snows a lot in Alaska."

"Let's move to Alaska, Poppy. You can buy me a sled."

"At the moment, that sounds like a good idea."

Spice watched him light his pipe, wondering aloud why he chose to live in a place where it never snowed.

His mind was on other things.

"Poppy, maybe we should ask God to make it snow."

He grunted. "I thought we agreed that God doesn't exist."

"Did I do that?"

"I thought we decided that if there were a God, things would have worked out differently for you and me."

"Poppy, I never decided that. I don't want us to be different." She patted his arm. "If things were different, you might not have me, so what would you do then?"

"I'd have a problem, wouldn't I?"

"A *big* problem." She stretched her arms out to indicate the size.

"You're a handful, gal."

She giggled.

Cicadas sang from the trees while crickets pitched in with their say-so. The breeze turned cooler. The moon, like a plump pumpkin, threw shadows from behind the treetops. Balls of fluffy cotton offered a polka-dot carpet across a field.

A car drove past. Booming drumbeats stereoed from the vehicle like the cannons of war. For a moment, even the breeze seemed to fade as a protest to the vile intrusion.

Elmer added fresh tobacco to his pipe.

"Poppy?"

"Huh?"

"I'll make a deal with you."

"And what will that cost me?"

"Nothing! Deals don't cost anything."

"Go ahead. Set me up."

She spread her hands. "This is the way it's supposed to work. You dip out the ice cream, and I'll eat it."

"That's a deal?"

"Poppy, don't you know anything? I can't do my part if you don't do yours."

"What do I get out of that deal?"

She spread her hands impatiently. "*You* get to go to the store and buy more ice cream when I eat it all up."

"Sounds more like a con job to me."

"Well, okay. Is it a deal?"

He went for the ice cream.

Gus Smith and Jo returned in the late afternoon three days later. Elmer, constantly on the alert, heard the car and ushered Spice down to the cellar.

He heard them arguing that night and eased up the steps to the door, hoping to learn how long they would be there.

"I don't like it," he heard Jo say.

Smith cursed. "I don't care what you don't like. It ain't far out of the way."

"It's too dangerous. We don't know those people."

"Look. I make the drop. They hand me my money, and we split. Nothing to it."

"It could be a set up, Gus."

"That's the chance you take in this business if you're going to get the big bucks. Where's a good place to hide the money and cargo?"

"In one of the barns, I suppose."

"Doesn't this place have a cellar?"

"The packhouse does. It's under a trap-door."

"My old man once said he thought there was a cellar under this house," said Smith.

"Well, he was wrong. Don't you think I'd know it if there was?"

"I got to make some calls. Fix us something to eat."

"I thought we were going out to eat."

"Are you crazy? I ain't hauling that stuff around in the car except when I have to."

"We can hide it tonight."

"In the dark? Look alive, kid. There's too much at stake to be fumbling around out there at night. We'll unload the surplus in the morning. It ain't gonna kill you to cook something!"

"How long will we be here?"

"Don't know yet. My contact was out. I left a message for him to call."

"Gus, I'm scared. Suppose that patrolman had stopped us?"

"Just because he was behind us all that distance doesn't mean he was suspicious or following us."

"I would have felt better if Spice had been with us," she said.

"Yeah, me, too. I need to find that old man and kid. Tell you what. Until we get the kid back, we'll use the back roads for a while. Just in case."

"I'd feel better if we did."

"Well, it shouldn't be too long before they're spotted. I just put the word out to some more people."

He couldn't hear Jo's reply.

"I'd use one of my brother's little brats, but there ain't no way anyone can control them. All mouth and screams."

"He'd let you?"

"Yeah. He'd be glad for someone to take them all off his hands. If I ever have any kids, I'm going to teach them to have some respect for their old man."

"Did you respect your father, Gus?"

"Pa?" He chuckled. "Pa was hard as nails and just as crazy. If you showed him any respect, he'd slap you through the door for being a sissy."

To help Spice pass the time, Elmer played silent games with her. He kept reminding her to remain quiet. So far, she'd made no noise, but he remained tense, knowing how quickly a child can forget.

Elmer awoke early as was his custom. After years of rising before the sun, it was difficult to change. He could count on his fingers the number of days he'd slept past sunup.

Hearing noise from above, he knew it wouldn't be long before they would be unloading the car. He quietly cracked the outside door and waited. Within the hour, he saw them carrying two large briefcases toward the packhouse. They did not tarry when they returned to the house. Within a few minutes, they drove off.

He waited another fifteen minutes.

Sliding the .45 pistol under his belt, he led the way up the stairs and through the closet. Elmer was in a hurry. He poured Spice a bowl of oat cereal.

"I want corn flakes," she said.

"They ate all the flakes. This stuff is pretty good."

"Not for me."

"Better eat it. I don't have time to cook anything."

"What about making a deal?"

"No deals this morning."

"Aw, Poppy!"

"All right. What's the deal?"

"I'll drink my milk, and then we can go to Shoney's."

"We might be seen."

"Well, you've got a gun, haven't you?"

"You would have me shoot up the neighborhood just so you can stuff yourself at Shoney's?"

"Yep."

"Eat."

Later, leaving the house at the back, he led Spice down behind the barns to the packhouse. If Spark knew Smith had been there and left, he might consider it a good time to search the place again.

Inside the packhouse he waited until his eyes became accustomed to the dull seepage of light through the cracks. The burlap bags appeared not to have been disturbed. He looked around the room. The cases could be tucked away most any place. The packhouse had not been cleaned out in years.

Fixing the general appearance of the bags covering the trap door in his mind, he carefully uncovered the door and pulled it open. With the flashlight scanning the cellar, he climbed down.

He found the cases behind several wooden crates Smith had thrown into the cellar. Hurriedly, he opened one. It was nearly full of large bills, neatly bundled with rubber bands.

The second case contained plastic bags filled with a white, powdery substance he took to be cocaine. He carried the cases out. Replacing the bags over the trap door, they left the packhouse and circled behind the outbuildings.

Entering the back door, he hurried to the cellar and shoved the cases into a crevice between the floor joists and the ground. Using his knife, he piled up dirt to hide them .

Now he had something with which to bait the trap-- something other than his granddaughter. He sat down and wiped perspiration from his face. After catching his breath, he filled his pipe.

"I hear a car, Poppy."

Chapter 15

Spark and the deputy searched the house a second time. Elmer watched from the access door under the porch as they hurried across the yard toward the barns. The deputy was not wearing his uniform. They went from building to building, spending considerable time in each. When Spark exited the packhouse, he called to the deputy. "Find anything?"

"Nothing."

They walked toward the house. "I know he hid it out here," said Spark.

"Tell you what," said Sam Black, the sheriff's deputy. "There's only one way we'll ever find it. Tonight I'll get the drug sniffer. If the stuff is here, he'll find it."

"Where the dope is, the money is, you can bet on that."

"I'll get the dog and meet you here after dark."

"We're in business," said Spark jubilantly. "Must be a fortune in kilos not to mention the cash he's got hid."

When the sound of the truck died, Elmer retrieved the two cases from under the floor joists. "We have to leave," he told Spice. He didn't know if the dog could scent out the drugs from above but couldn't take any chances. He didn't want to think about what would happen to him or Spice if they were discovered in the cellar with the cases.

Where could they go?

Leaving the cellar, he made certain the door was secured. It was the only place that was really safe. In time, the searchers or Smith might discover the "dungeon." He hoped to end the matter before that happened.

He debated going to Rastus Wolfe's house but decided against it, not being sure he could trust anyone.

Elmer hurried Spice along. When they reached the truck, he placed the two cases between them and drove out of the woods. The only thing he could do was drive straight to town and hope Smith's spotters wouldn't see him.

Turning in at the used car lot, he parked the truck behind a line of cars, took out the cases, and hurried to his Dodge parked near the paint shed. He threw the cases in the trunk.

At first, he thought someone was following him out of town, but the truck turned onto a side street, and he took a deep breath of relief. Spice started to rise up off the floor. "Keep down!"

"Little people aren't supposed to sit on the floor, Poppy."

"You can get up when we're off the highway."

A state patrol car fell in behind him. Elmer slowed down even though he was traveling well under the speed limit. The patrolman pulled around him and continued up the road.

He turned onto the dirt road leading along the edge of the swamp. After crossing a sagging and creaking wooden bridge, he entered a narrow strip of road seldom traveled and eased the car through a close passage of overhanging tree limbs and vines.

After a quarter of a mile, a small clearing opened up.

"That's Miss Mollie's house!" exclaimed Spice. "I didn't know we were coming here."

Miss Mollie came out onto the porch, peering from under a polka-dot bonnet. "That be ye, Elmer?"

"It's me, Miss Mollie."

"Well, ain't this a surprise! It's the little spicy young'un, too. Y'all git down."

Dark clouds hovered over the swamp. Elmer smelled rain in the air. A roll of thunder applauded in the distance. The woman, her long dress catching the gust of breeze, appeared to Elmer to have stepped through a time warp, emerging from the late 1800's. The old house lent credence to the illusion.

"Ye fetchin' me troubles agin, Elmer?"

"I hope not, Miss Mollie."

"No matter. Y'all come on in. I was about cooking supper, I was."

He looked around. The barn, standing askew on deteriorating pillars, gaped at him from its sagging door. The adjoining wagon shed, propped with a pole, sheltered a weathered one-horse wagon, dilapidated with a missing shaft and broken spokes.

The hound lay sleeping under the twisted chinaberry tree. Elmer wondered if the dog had moved since his last visit. Lightning streaked farther down the swamp. The sky clapped its thunder. "Fixin' to let in," said the woman. "Fixin' to fill a bottomless bucket, 'pears to me."

"That'd be some downpour," said Elmer.

Miss Mollie cackled. Spice slipped around her grandfather, holding onto his back pocket. "She laughs funny," whispered Spice.

He followed the woman inside. She busied at the wood stove. "How's fatback, biscuits and taters suit y'all?"

"Sounds good to me," said Elmer.

Spice looked up at him. "You'll like it," Elmer said.

"I got a chocolate cake in the safe," said Miss Mollie, squinting down at Spice.

Spice grinned.

The woman ran her eyes to Elmer. "Don't ye believe in little gals wearing dresses? Seems to me she was wearing them work overalls the last time."

"I don't like dresses," said Spice, eyeing the cake in the strange-looking cabinet the woman called a "safe".

"Yeah, modern gals got strange ideas. Even the little sprouts."

The kitchen smelled of baking biscuits, strips of porkside frying, and boiling coffee. The woman cut thin slices of potatoes and dropped a handful in hot grease. "I don't eat fancy, but it's a pleasurable fillin'."

"Does it taste good?" said Spice.

"Depends on how hungry ye be, Spicey."

"I am hungry," said Spice. She ventured over to a small table near the door. "What's that?" She pointed to a fruit jar.

"That be some preserves I put up last fall. Tastes good on hot biscuits."

Spice frowned.

Large drops of rain hit the tin roof. Jagged streaks of lightning played haphazardly among the higher trees of the swamp, streaking earthward frequently. Thunder shook the small house.

"Tis the Master at play, it is," said Miss Mollie.

"Or plain old nature," Elmer offered.

The woman nodded. "The differences be the same. He done made nature like He made us." She withdrew a pan of biscuits from the oven.

"Shouldn't be standing near that stove with lightning so close," warned Elmer.

"I wouldn't if nature was in control." She looked over her steel-rim glasses at him. The wrinkled face provided a grin. "That be the difference between us, Elmer. Ye shy from nature. I shy to the good Lord above."

"Each to his own," said Elmer dryly.

The woman moved the frying pan of side meat from the stove and wiped the apron over her face. "The wonder of it is that a body can reach your age without ever discovering the whys of nature. 'Pears to me ye'd done stumble onto the truth by accident, if nothing else."

"You going to start preaching to me again, Miss Mollie?"

She cackled. "Lordy, no. I'm fer folks keeping their religion and politics to themselves. I just tell ye what the truth be. If ye can't swallow it, then maybe yer belly wouldn't hold it nohow."

Elmer puffed his pipe, looking out through the rusty screen door. The rain continued pelting the roof. A bolt cracked overhead. The woman ignored it, turning the potato slices.

Spice leaned against his leg, watching the woman, her green eyes following her every movement. "You know something, Miss Mollie?"

Miss Mollie leaned over her. The wrinkled hands of labor held close to the child's face. "Ye can call me 'Granny.' "

"You know what, Granny?"

"What?"

"Your house smells good."

The old woman smiled. "If ye eat a good supper, I be having a treat for ye--a piece of candy I be saving."

Spice smiled broadly. She reached up and hugged the woman. Miss Mollie patted her head. "Ye be a good young'un."

The bulk stood in the doorway, filling the space with his own. He clutched a thick, long pole. Spice gasped, moving closer to Elmer.

A black beard hid most of the face. The wide-brimmed black hat drooped rain-soaked over his eyes. He looked down at Elmer as he walked over to the stove, the heels of large boots dragging the floor. The man's head almost touched the ceiling. Elmer had never seen such a large man. The thick muscles of his huge arms bulged under the wet plaid shirt. His overalls were drenched. He reached for a biscuit, and Miss Mollie hit him on the arm with a spatula. "Git away from there!"

He laughed. It was more of a roar. Spice hugged Elmer's leg.

Slowly, he turned dark, deep-set eyes to study Elmer and Spice.

"Elmer, this here be my grandson, Elijah," said Miss Mollie.

Elmer took the extended hand. It was like trying to grasp a ham. Elijah looked down at Spice. He swung her up in the air.

"Poppy?"

"I won't hurt you, girl, "Elijah said, his voice nearly booming in Spice's ear.

She pushed against his chest. "Poppy!"

Elijah placed her in Elmer's lap. He sat at the table, his eyes holding on Elmer. "Saw you and the girl in the swamp the other day. Wondered if you were going to make it out."

"I didn't see you," said Elmer.

"No one ever sees me," he said pointedly. "Not unless I want them to."

Elmer had heard stories of a huge man; some even said he was a giant, roaming the swamps, especially along the waterways, poaching alligators, and eating the meat.

"How's the alligator business?" said Elmer.

Elijah shrugged. "It's a living. It lets me do what I please."

"It's agin the law," reminded Miss Mollie.

"I only take what I need to live on."

"That don't make it right," she returned.

Elijah studied Elmer. "You're in a lot of danger."

Elmer returned his gaze. "I know."

"Your coming here puts my grandma at risk."

Was he warning him? "I had no other place to go."

"Then you come to my place."

"Where's that?"

"I'll show you."

Miss Mollie placed the food on the table. "He lives deep in the swamp. Way down on the river."

The rain came down harder. Lightning flashed continuously in the darkened skies. The light bulb hanging above glowed off the bearded face. "I don't trust you," said Elmer.

Elijah smiled. "Does it make any difference?"

Elmer thought about it. "No. I guess not. It would take a poor excuse of a man to harm an old man and a little girl."

Elijah's expression, what of it he could see, didn't change. He looked at Spice and back to him. "We'll eat and then we go."

"In this weather?"

"Yes, if it doesn't clear by then."

The rain stopped. The night was as black as Elmer had ever seen. "Wouldn't it be better if we waited until daylight?"

"Don't worry about it. Just follow me," said Elijah, going out onto the porch. He lit an old Coleman lantern, turning it down low.

"I have to get something out of the car," said Elmer.

He knew Elijah was watching him. Elmer took the .45 from the glove compartment and stuck it under his belt. From the trunk he retrieved the two cases and slammed the lid shut.

"If you have what I think you've got there, you're asking for a lot of trouble."

"You seem to know a lot of what's going on for one who lives in the swamp," said Elmer.

A hand rested on his shoulder. "I know that gun won't do you much good where we're going. I know you're carrying something that will bring killers and trailing dogs to the swamp."

"That's a fair summation."

"It's a fool thing," the swamper said, taking the cases from him. "I'll carry them. You'll have hard enough time keeping up as it is."

Elijah swept Spice up into his arm. "Follow me."

Elmer could see nothing except the dim glow of the lantern. He followed the man through a part of the swamp where he'd never been. A mist hovered over the ground; as the clouds dispersed, moonlight filtered through the fog like a scene from a mystic dream. Night sounds, some by animals, some by birds, and some by insects, made a strange orchestra.

In a rough clearing, jagged stubs of tree trunks protruded above the ground-hugging mist like ghostly sentinels. Tall, sharp-blade grass tore at Elmer's legs. An alligator grunted nearby. Farther off, another replied. Hanging from an overhead branch, a snake hissed. Elijah smacked the serpent with his pole, a weapon in its own right. Elmer leaned low to pass under the limb.

A panther to the east paused in his hunt to growl a warning.

Deeper into the swamp they trekked, sometimes their heads just above the thick mist. Often it completely engulfed them. Still, the moon played out its role, seeming to ignite the vapor as if it were some sort of luminous gas.

"Poppy?" called Spice."

"Right behind you, honey."

Elijah plodded on, the big boots crushing through the grass and brush.

"Quicksand ahead," warned Elijah. "Step where I step."

Elmer obeyed.

An hour later, Elijah paused on a slight rise. He put Spice down. She grabbed Elmer around the leg. "Reckon you could use a rest about here," he told Elmer.

"I could." Elmer leaned against a tree. "How much farther?"

"We'll soon be there. The river's just ahead."

"You live alone?"

"As alone as you can get."

Elmer didn't trust Elijah. But what choice did he have? He continued to follow him through the mist of a hot, fall night, wondering when his nightmare would end.

After what seemed hours, they came to the river, a shallow, slow-moving dark water with wide banks. Elijah turned up the waterway for a half-mile, changing directions where a creek joined the wider flow. Fifteen minutes later, they entered a tall grove of oaks, their limbs spread like the thick arms of an octopus. The ground underneath had been cleared of undergrowth.

In the middle of the area, Elmer saw the house. He didn't believe his own eyes.

Chapter 16

The log house rested on post pillars ten feet above the ground. Elmer estimated the structure to be thirty-four feet long and almost as wide. As the morning sun broke through the overhead foliage, he saw that the shingles were handmade from large cypress trees. In fact, the logs and pillars were of cypress. Going closer and surveying the structure with a carpenter's eye, he had to admire the work of the man holding his sleeping granddaughter. "I see some fair craft here."

Elijah nodded. A slight grin broke through the beard. He nodded for Elmer to follow him. They climbed the ladder going up through the floor of the deck on the front of the cabin. Elijah pushed open the trap door. "I favor this method over steps. Keeps out varmints and snakes."

Elmer could appreciate that.

The interior surprised him even more.

It was two large rooms. Paintings of swamp animals and scenes adorned the log walls. One huge painting depicted a large, bearded man wrestling a huge alligator. Elmer decided it was a self-portrait.

The hide of a massive rattlesnake took up much of the wall behind a double bed.

Elmer slowly took it all in. Two powerful-looking compound bows stood in a corner near the door. The quivers held arrows with razor-sharp, steel hunting points.

"You are proficient with those, I imagine," said Elmer.

Elijah nodded. He placed Spice on the bed.

Elmer noticed the place appeared spotless. White mortar mix made the chinking between the large logs. Wide, wooden floorboards maintained a high gloss. Pole beams, shaved to a shiny surface, stretched across the width of the rooms.

The table and tools of a painter occupied the space near a large window. "You surprise me, Elijah."

"Why? Because I paint?"

"That, among other things. I'm certainly no critic, but I'd say you are very good at what you do."

"I am."

"How'd you get the furniture and building materials in here?"

"Some by raft down the river. Some I carried in on my back."

"That took some doing."

"Doesn't everything?"

Elijah crossed the room to the kitchen area. He put the cases on a shelf. He turned to Elmer. "Let me guess. One contains money. The other cocaine."

"That's right."

Elijah studied him. "You play a dangerous game, old man."

"Do you know Gus Smith?"

"I do. I also knew your daughter, Jo. The little girl is her daughter, isn't she?"

Elmer nodded. "How long can we stay here?"

"I haven't decided. I don't like the idea of getting mixed up with something that doesn't concern me, especially dope trafficking."

"I understand. We'll get out of your way in a couple of days."

Elijah scratched his beard. "How much money is there in the case?"

"I don't know. Probably a hundred thousand or more."

Elijah whistled. "That'll bring them out of the woodwork."

He built a fire in the stove. "They may trace you here. I'm concerned about the little girl. What's her name anyway?"

"Spice."

"Mind if I paint her?"

"Of course not."

"It's been a long time since I tried a portrait. I was never pleased with my subjects."

Elmer studied the painting of Miss Mollie hanging on the far wall. "You certainly caught her spirit."

"She was the exception. Always will be."

"Where'd you know Jo?"

"Back in grammar school. I doubt if she would remember me except as a big, overgrown clod."

"Strange that Jo never mentioned you."

"Not really. Why would she? I was too self-conscious to do anything except stay in the background. I was too big for anyone to poke fun at, to my face. Anyway, my folks moved to North Carolina when I was twelve."

"About three years ago folks around here started talking about a swamp bogeyman," advised Elmer.

"That's when I came back here to do my work, believing it was the best place to live off the land while I tested my abilities. Needlessly to say, I probably encouraged the speculation that I was some kind of freak. Keeps people away."

When Elijah set the meal on the table, Elmer awoke Spice. He tasted a strange but a pleasant course. "What is this?"

"Fresh meat and swamp salad. What else? Without electricity, there is no refrigerator. Without refrigeration, I take what is fresh."

Elmer wished he hadn't asked.

"It's good," said Spice. "Can I have some more?"

"May I have some more," corrected Elijah. "This stuff will make you grow."

"I asked first," said Spice. "You're big enough already; don't you know that?"

Elijah filled her plate. He looked at his watch. "You two can wash the dishes. I have an appointment up river."

He returned Elmer's gaze. "Don't worry, Mr. Goodhand. I'm not going to mention that you two are here. This has nothing to do with anyone who associates with Gus Smith or his crowd. It's hide business."

"Poaching can be serious business."

"The immediate world around us is serious business, Mr. Goodhand, as you already know. I take only enough hides to sustain me with simple wants. I leave no signs of my illegal activities. The swamp is crowded with alligators. I merely thin them from time to time."

"The state boys would see it differently."

"No doubt, but I've never seen them in here."

He picked up one of the bows and a quiver of arrows. "I won't be gone long."

"I hope not. I doubt if I could get out of here on my own."

"It would be difficult."

It was a freakish place. He sat out on the deck with Spice, contemplating the surroundings. It was deceptively cool among the large oaks. The sun filtered through the tall branches without even so much a hint of heat. The breeze actually had a chill to it.

He held the pipe stem between his teeth, wondering about the man who sought such solitude in which to live and work. He was not only an artist with a brush and canvas but equally adept with his hands. The house revealed a certain love of work, a craftsman able to do all things to perfection.

Elijah returned in the afternoon, emerging from the thick undergrowth as silently as a serpent in stalk of prey. He at once began work on Spice's portrait.

Spice, at first, was reluctant to sit still. But it was soon evident that Elijah had a way with children, teasing and coaxing, until Spice was obedient to his every wish. Even, it seemed to Elmer, Elijah would see how long she could sit without batting an eye in order to win the "game".

Elijah kept the sessions short, not pushing his luck. He rewarded her with tasty tidbits from a cabinet. Elmer was relieved to see they were cookies from a box.

For two days Elmer watched Elijah work. He allowed Spice to inspect his work from time to time. During each inspection she provided instructions on how to improve the portrait. Elijah seemed to take her criticism seriously. "Really," he would say. "Do you honestly think I should do that?"

"I think so."

"Well, I don't know. Don't you think that would make you too pretty?"

"Nope. Poppy said I was pretty."

"What do you think about your poppy?" urged Elijah. She shrugged. "I don't know. He hasn't paid me all my dollars."

"Is he cheating you?" boomed Elijah.

She giggled, nodding. "Yep."

"Maybe I ought to beat him up."

Her hands flew to her hips. She narrowed her eyes at him. "You do, and you'll be sorry! My poppy will stuff you in the ground!"

"I wish I could capture that look," said Elijah.

Spice looked at Elmer. "When *do* I get my other dollars, Poppy?"

"I didn't know I owed you any."

"Poppy, you're just trying to forget!" She held up three fingers. "I think you owe me that many."

"All right. When we get home, I'll pay you. I might be able to find a dollar."

She looked at her raised fingers and then at him. "That many, Poppy. Look. That many."

"All right."

She stood down off the stool to inspect the painting. "That's better," she advised.

"Do you think you'll be able to keep Jo from going back to prison, Mr. Goodhand?" asked Elijah.

Elmer glanced at him. The man seemed occupied with his canvas. "I don't know," Elmer said. "I hope so."

"They'll eventually catch Smith. When they do, she's caught. If you can hold onto that money over there, you might hire a lawyer smart enough to get her off."

"I'm not interested in that money except for one thing."

Elijah glanced his way. "Burying Smith?"

"What happens to him will be his own doing."

"That's a big order. Smith's no fool."

"Where did you get to know him so well?"

"I don't. Not personally. All I know about him and his operation is what I hear."

"He's a scoundrel."

"He is. Have you thought about what could happen if that money and dope isn't his? Suppose it belongs to the big boys? You could find yourself dealing with a mob."

"I've thought about that."

"It could get real rough, you know. Have you any idea what the value of that cocaine is?"

"I don't know anything about that stuff."

"Well, judging by the weight of the case, I'd say if it were pure stuff, it would have a street value of over a quarter of a million dollars."

"I didn't know it was gold."

"Regardless of who it belongs to, they wouldn't hesitate to kill for it."

"You seem to know a lot about drugs, mobs, and the like."

"I try to keep up with what's going on." He went over and tilted Spice's head for a different angle.

Elmer watched him stroke the canvas lightly. "What are you leading up to, Elijah?"

"Simply this. Risking your life is one thing. Risking the life of Jo and Spice is another. I could return the cases to Smith. It might save you a lot of grief."

"Can't. I need them."

Elijah paused, studying him. "I could take them."

Elmer's hand fell to the butt of the pistol in his waistband. "You might. You might not."

Chapter 17

Elijah's slow smile left Elmer feeling uncertain. He recalled the man's warning that here, in this place, the gun would be of no particular advantage.

Elijah put aside the brushes. Elmer stepped over to the door, his back to the man. A feeling of hopelessness swarmed over him. He didn't trust Elijah. There were too many unanswered questions. The man seemed to know a lot about what was happening to only have a passing interest in what went on outside the swamp.

"Smith's connections will kill to recover what's in those cases," reminded Elijah. "If he doesn't beat them to it."

"I know what I'm up against," said Elmer.

"Then you know you've got nowhere to turn for help-- except possibly to me."

"I haven't asked you for help, have I?"

"That's true."

Elmer walked out onto the deck. The air felt heavy. A hawk sent a shrill warning from high in the trees. The sun penetrated an opening in the overhead foliage, dashing spots of light here and there like scattered rain drops. Elmer sat on a bench made from a half log. He packed his pipe.

He couldn't decide what to do next. He was tired of hiding and tired of running and wished there were a simple way out.

Elmer wondered if he were merely postponing the inevitable by staying at Elijah's swamp retreat. Since delaying the situation could increase the possibility that they would be caught in the destructive web, perhaps going to the Federal authorities and letting the law take its course would provide the only way to protect Spice.

"Poppy?"

"Yeah?"

She sat on the bench beside him. "I wish we would go home."

"We will."

"When?"

"When it's safe."

The green eyes held his. "You know something, Poppy?"

He responded as always.

"Big people aren't supposed to run away from home."

"They aren't?"

She shook her head.

"Well, before you know it, we'll be running back home."

She smiled. "And never leave again?"

He grunted.

"You sound like an alligator, Poppy."

"I feel like I'm part alligator with all the time we're spending in the swamp."

She giggled. "Me, too." Spice tried a course grunt. "How's that sound?'

"Scary."

She chuckled loudly.

Elijah came out. He carried a bow. A sheathed knife hung from his belt. "I'm going to look around."

"Expecting visitors?" asked Elmer.

"You never know. The swamp has its own way of announcing trespassers."

"I haven't heard anything."

"You wouldn't. Once you've lived in it for a while, you begin to learn its methods of communication."

"Could be someone fishing the river."

"Hardly," said Elijah, opening the door in the floor. "The river's not navigable this far in."

"Don't you use a boat to get out?"

"Only part of the way. The river is blocked at Bogeyman Creek with sand bars and fallen trees."

Carrying his pole, he disappeared through a wall of vines and brush. Elmer knew where Bogeyman Creek joined the river. He'd killed a large buck in that area twenty years ago. Back then you could travel the entire length of the river through the swamp if your boat were a small one. He had a better idea where he was now. Snake Island lay off to the east. A stretch of treacherous quicksand blocked any direct travel from Elijah's cabin to his farm.

The trouble with traveling strange areas of the swamp at night was that you quickly lost all sense of direction. It was tricky, at best, even when you knew the swamp. He had been amazed at the sureness with which Elijah had journeyed through the maze at night.

Elmer had noticed that there was not the slightest indication of a path leading to the cabin. One could come within a few feet of the place and never know of its existence.

Elijah appeared too cautious for a man who merely wished to escape people. Of course, there was the poaching thing, but how many rangers would care to venture so far into a jungle on the slim chance of catching someone who killed a few alligators?

What had caused the man to go looking for a trespasser armed with arrows and a knife? Was he hiding from something? Had he told the truth about the swamp's communicating its strange, mystic messages?

He remembered that years ago, after spending time in the swamp, he, too, felt he could read the feel and sounds of this jungle. It was conceivable that one living in the swamp could develop that sense. After all, animals, birds, and even the thick air itself, could, when disturbed, send out alarms.

The afternoon dragged on, the sun yet fighting to find a way to filter through to the deck. Occasionally, a sprinkle of rays succeeded only to be broken and scattered by the breeze disturbing the upper branches.

The life of the swamp geared for the approaching night with their peculiar movements and sounds. Shadows played a ritual, shifting playfully in overlapping layers until the gray of dusk settled the game.

A bobcat signaled that he was on the prowl. A gator from near the river grunted that he, too, was alert. Three wild hogs, one a boar with curved tusks, ventured into the clearing searching for food. Not far away wild dogs barked. The hogs jerked still, ears cocked while they tested the air for scent.

As if by signal, crickets surrounding the cabin called for attention. A screech owl joined the melee. Spice moved closer to him. "Poppy?"

"Yeah?"

"Did Elijah get lost?"

"I doubt it. He should be getting back pretty soon."

Ten minutes later Elijah returned carrying two rabbits. He said nothing. He went inside and built a fire in the stove. It wasn't long before Elmer caught the aroma of coffee and meat frying. Spice followed Elmer inside. "Can I help?" he said.

"No."

"You find your trespassers?"

"It was nothing, not anything that concerns you."

"Then there is someone out there."

"I said it didn't concern you."

Elmer wasn't too sure.

Elijah poured a cup of coffee and handed it to Elmer, their eyes meeting. Elmer tasted the coffee. "We'll be leaving in the morning."

"Do you know the way out?"

"I can manage."

"You'll have to carry the little girl quite some ways. Can you handle that, too? And what about the two cases over there? How will you transport them?"

Elmer sipped coffee. He didn't have the answers. "That rabbit looks done."

They ate in silence. The lamp in the center of the table cast a diluted glow inside the cabin. Foxes yelped nearby; an owl argued back from a high perch.

"You could leave the girl or the cases with me," said Elijah.

"I don't trust you."

"That does present a problem, doesn't it?"

"I'm going with Poppy," announced Spice.

"You could help us part of the way out," suggested Elmer.

Elijah shook his head. "Helping you means seeing you getting deeper into something that can only end one way. Whatever you have planned can only be a foolish gesture on your part. You can do nothing to change things."

"I'm still going to try."

"And get your fool self killed in the process."

Elmer went to the stove and refilled their coffee cups. "What would you do in my place?" he asked the big man.

Elijah scratched his beard. "To be honest with you, I don't know. I guess I'd concentrate on staying alive."

"I want to leave Spice with Miss Mollie for a few days," Elmer said, lighting his pipe.

"I told you I didn't want you involving her."

"I know you did, but there's no other choice."

"It's out of the question."

He lay on his pallet on the hard floor that night searching for an answer. Spice slept on blankets nearby. Over in the bed Elijah snored loudly, competing with the myriad of noises from outside. Elmer couldn't quite bring himself to trust Elijah. He didn't know why. It was nothing except a feeling.

His feelings--how many times had they misled him? Could he even trust himself anymore to do the right thing? Nothing he tried seemed to work out right, and everything made matters worse. After twisting and turning most of the night, he finally made up his mind.

Chapter 18

Dense fog lay as a dingy blanket over the swamp, its penetrating dampness forming drops of water on trees and underbrush. Elmer went out onto the deck and shook the dried mud from Spice's overalls. As they readied to leave, he found her cap and stuck it on her head.

Elijah looked on in silence as Elmer took down the two cases and opened them, checking the contents.

"Your best route is across the bogs," advised Elijah when they started out. "If you bend too far north, you'll end up in quicksand country."

"From what direction did we come from Miss Mollie's?"

Elijah followed them out onto the deck. He pointed eastward. "But don't go to her place," he warned.

"Just wanted to make sure of my directions."

Elijah handed him a canteen. "Better take this. You won't find water fit to drink between here and your place."

Elmer hung the canteen over his shoulder.

"I'll say it again," said Elijah. "You're being a fool taking those cases. You'll be worn through before you're a third of the way out."

"I wish you luck with your paintings," said Elmer. "I sure wouldn't mind having that one of Spice."

"It's the best thing I've ever done," admitted Elijah.

He traveled parallel to the river until the waterway curved southward, carrying Spice through the tall grass and low tangle of thorny vines. With his pocketknife, he cut a strip from his shirttail, tied the ends to the briefcase handles, and hung them from his shoulder. An hour in the heat sapped his strength. Swamp dogs howled to the west. It might be a pack on a hunt. Elmer pushed on, leading Spice through a less hazardous area where the tall grass thinned out.

Under the shade of a large poplar tree, Elmer paused to rest, sitting on the thick layer of leaves. Spice sat down beside him. He wiped her perspiring face with his handkerchief. He carefully studied the area.

How easily it would be for him to become lost here. Everything looked the same. Cypresses appeared as long utility poles with leaves reaching for the sun. Their bell-bottom trunks balanced the whole in shallow, soupy water. Naked stems of limbless trees, having died from rising backwaters, were jagged exclamation points to the savagery of the environment.

An eagle watched a gathering of large rats from his perch atop a stem. A circle of buzzards rode the rising currents. A hawk screamed toward the rodents. Black birds took to the air. The dogs sounded closer. Elmer struggled to his feet.

Later, he saw a king snake and a timber rattler engaged in combat. He bypassed the war zone, carrying Spice through a stretch of tall grass. Blindly, he proceeded, trusting to luck.

He had to detour around a beaver pond. Gnats swarmed worse than usual. A large alligator and several smaller ones sunned on the dam. Elmer paused, his hand on the pistol butt. He thought he heard a movement in the brush.

He wiped a sleeve across his forehead.

"I'm thirsty, Poppy."

Elmer held the canteen while she drank. Humidity thickened the still air. The wet shirt stuck to his back. He heard the swamp dogs again.

Later, following a deer trail, he had Spice walk behind him. She complained of being tired. He urged her on. "We'll find a spot to rest up ahead," he said.

The ground sloped gradually upward. Elmer turned off the trail, pushing through a thicket. The area looked vaguely familiar. He paused at the crest to look around. He knew exactly where he was now. The hard part, the bogs, lay south, the direction they must go to reach home.

A breeze brushed against his face. Overhead, the leaves rustled to a slight disturbance. A deer darted into the small clearing. He wondered if the dogs were on the doe's trail. He hoped not.

The short rest revived him. Walking among the large sprawling oaks, he felt certain this was where he'd seen the hollow tree when they were running from Smith.

He found it where the underbrush thickened and poked a stick in the trunk's cavity, making certain no snake was holed up in the hollow. Satisfied, he slid the cases in, gathered leaves and dumped them on top.

Spanish moss draped from the thick limbs of the old oak like trimmers of faded rags. Higher up, a hive of bees manufactured honey in a smaller cavity.

"Are you rested enough to move on?" Elmer said.

She nodded. "I suppose, if I have to."

Leaving the rise, they entered thick undergrowth. The humid air, motionless and heavy, made breathing difficult. He paused more frequently now, catching quick periods of rest. Later, as the sun escaped to the west, they crossed more places where he had to carry Spice.

They finally reached the bogs. His muscles ached. He worried about the dogs. The ferocious mongrels would attack for the mere sake of killing.

There was no choice but to carry Spice. The tall, wicked blades of the grass were the least of the dangers. Snakes and alligators often favored the grass for hunting prey. The ground shifted under his weight. The grass momentarily kept his feet from sinking farther into the soft earth. He paused for his breath. The solitude seemed to grasp one with viciousness. A crow cawed a warning. The innocent whistle of a quail veiled a dark secret.

The pounding splash of an alligator's tail nearby meant death to some living creature. Death hung in the air like the odor of black, stagnant water. One's nostrils became filled with the brackishness of it.

He stopped to rest, putting Spice down. Remembering the last time they were in the bogs and how close he had come to passing out, he cautioned himself not to overdo. If the dogs crossed their path, they would probably follow the scent. They must hurry.

He lifted Spice. "I can walk, Poppy."

"Not in here."

He quickened his pace. The dogs *were* coming. They must reach the trees and be out of the bogs for here there was nothing to climb or hide behind.

He rushed when footing would permit, no longer feeling the jabs and pricks of the grass. He forgot about snakes and gators. He had only one purpose in mind--find a tree!

The dogs came on. It was a hunt!

Elmer stumbled, falling. He lay for a moment, sucking in air. Spice helped him up. She had somehow landed on her feet.

"Honey, I can't carry you any farther."

"I can walk, Poppy."

"Follow in my steps," he cautioned, leading the way.

Was the light fading? He squinted his eyes. What had he done, risking Spice to this--again? Was he losing his mind?

A dog howled behind them.

Elmer tried to run.

He wondered if they would make it.

The grass thinned under his feet. He looked up, his eyes burning, washed in sweat. A hundred feet before them, stood a lone tree. He pushed Spice in front of him.

His ears felt strange, pounding out hollow, tight sounds. With great effort, he threw one foot in front of the other.

"Hurry, Poppy!"

One foot. Now the other foot.

Jabs of pain shot through his head.

"Poppy! Hurry!"

One foot. Now another foot. Another --

"Poppy!"

He fell against the tree, his lungs retching, his eyes blurred, the bushes moving, shifting in a fuzzy motion. Somewhere he found the strength to shove Spice up the tree. "Grab the limb! Pull yourself up. Climb higher!"

She reached a safe height. Elmer pulled the pistol, jacked a round into the chamber and waited.

Sleeving his face, he blinked to clear his eyes. With legs trembling, he leaned against the tree to steady himself. Spice sat on a limb above him hugging the trunk.

"Poppy?"

"You hold on tight."

Even if the tree had been large enough to support them both, he would not have had the strength to climb it. He waited, the automatic cocked.

Anger filled him--anger against himself. He'd brought a child to this! His stupidity might cost them both their lives!

He counted eight dogs as they formed a circle, their fangs displayed. A huge white male appeared to be the leader. Elmer withdrew his pocketknife and with shaking hands struggled to open the blade. To him a pocketknife was a tool and like all of his cutting tools, Elmer kept the blade razor sharp.

His vision cleared. The throbbing in his ears subsided. He drew a deep breath and stared into the dark eyes of the big white. Should he shoot him now or wait? Would a shot bring on an attack or scare the others away?

He didn't know what he should do.

They growled. The hair stood along their backs. He saw their fangs displayed behind snarling lips.

The sun threatened to set to a bleak, gray sky. Somewhere, fixed between the snarls, a cougar growled.

He heard Spice snubbing.

The white mongrel moved in closer.

"Poppy?"

He heard it as a whisper, the tiny voice strained with fear.

He wanted to reply, to reassure her. He couldn't. His mouth was too dry. He remembered having such a fear during a killing spree on a front line during a war. It was a fear that prepared the mind and body. With it came a strange strength.

He risked looking up at his granddaughter. "Whatever happens, you stay up there," he said, surprised his voice sounded calm.

She snubbed, nodding.

The dogs tightened the circle. Elmer could smell them, the stench burning his nostrils. He kept his eye on the white dog as he crept forward. Behind Elmer, a red mongrel prepared to leap.

The scream came from above his head.

Chapter 19

Fangs bared and eyes glaring with deathly purpose, the beast lunged for his throat. The bullet slammed the dog in the chest, hitting like a sledgehammer, knocking him back. Even as he fired, Elmer realized the red mongrel behind him had launched his attack. He swung around to fire. The .45 shattered the air as the dog reached to clamp jaws onto Elmer's thigh. The slug burst the skull. Elmer fired at another, missing. The German Shepherd came for him, leaping from ten feet away.

He heard the swish, the fine splicing of air, the cutting thud, the puncturing of bowels. The German Shepherd fell at Elmer's feet, the arrow protruding all the way through.

The others sprang to attack with ferociousness. A huge, screaming bulk plowed through the brush, wading into the mass of snarling, gnashing killers, and swinging a six-foot long, three-inch thick pole.

Elmer aimed for a dog on the fringes of the battle and fired. The bullet rolled the animal into a howling heap. He heard the crushing of skulls and bones. One dog limped off, howling. Others lay strewn at Elijah's feet. The one animal left standing made a lunge for Elijah. The man caught him by the jaws. Holding the clawing canine at arm length, he ripped the mouth apart, tearing it like a rotten sheet.

It had all happened so quickly. Elijah lifted Spice from the tree and held her close, soothing her with a deep calm voice.

"Were you bit?" he asked Elmer.

Elmer shook his head.

"Come on," said Elijah. "I know a good place to make night camp."

Carrying Spice, Elijah led the way through the trees, across a small stream and through a mass of vines. Eventually, as full darkness settled over the swamp, they reached a section of higher ground.

Elijah cleaned away a spot with his foot and built a fire. He took bread and cookies from his backpack. Elmer watched as he handed Spice her choice of the cookies.

"You've been following us all the way?"

Elijah ignored the question. He handed Elmer a handful of oatmeal cookies.

"You've fought dogs before," said Elmer

The man nodded. "If you had shot the white and red when they first circled, the others would have scattered."

"From or toward me?"

Elijah chuckled. "Good question."

"Why didn't you shoot sooner?" Elmer wondered aloud.

"A bow doesn't make a bang. Killing a member of a pack with an arrow could bring on an attack, whereas the sound of a shot often frightens them away."

"That's proven stuff, I suppose?"

"In part."

"You still haven't answered my question," reminded Elmer. "How long had you been following us?"

"Does it make any difference? You both are alive."

"It makes a difference if you saw where I hid the cases."

"Well, you'll just have to wonder about that."

"I know where it is," said Spice. "But I'm not telling."

"Why?" said Elijah. "Do you think I would steal them?"

Spice shrugged. "Probably no. Probably yes."

"The important thing," said Elmer, "is we're still alive. I can thank you for that. I hate to think what would have happened if you hadn't shown up when you did."

Elijah put a cookie in his mouth. "I tagged along because I felt responsible for you both. After all, I'm the one who took you so deep into the swamp." He added sticks to the fire. "Mr. Goodhand, you have a penchant for trouble. It follows you around like a dark cloud. I'm wondering how you've managed to live so long."

"My poppy doesn't have a penny for trouble!"

Elmer lit his pipe. "Perhaps it's because of the strange characters I'm always running into."

Something moved through the brush behind Elmer. Elijah fitted an arrow to his bow. "Some beast has probably decided to add to your troubles."

A pair of big, glaring eyes stared back at Elmer from the thick growth. Elmer grunted. He moved to where his back wouldn't be exposed, where he wouldn't be in the path of an arrow. "You're pretty good with that thing, by the way."

"If I weren't, you wouldn't be here eating my cookies."

Elmer threw wood on the fire. The life of the swamp chirped, snorted, and growled around them. Spice moved close to Elmer. A scream, sounding like a woman in distress, split the night from afar.

"Sounds like a panther," said Elmer.

"It is. I've seen him. A big black devil."

It had been years since Elmer had seen a panther of any size and thought they'd all been killed. The scream was enough to freeze the blood. He hated to hear it. He noticed Elijah still held the arrow in position. Another pair, equally upsetting, joined the pair of eyes in the thicket. Elmer was glad they had a good fire going.

"Poppy, I'm sleepy."

Elijah untied the bedroll from his backpack and stretched it out. "I thought you'd be needing this, young lady."

"Thank you," said Spice lying down. "I need my sleep."

"Where did you learn to be such a calm little thing?"

"My poppy."

She was soon comfortably asleep.

Elijah looked at Elmer smoking his pipe. "You any idea what you got in that bundle?" he said, indicating Spice.

Elmer threw a fresh stick on the fire. Sparks drifted skyward. He said nothing.

"Yeah," grunted the big man. "You know."

"It's my age," Elmer said softly. "I'm afraid of dying and leaving her all alone."

"Then why do you court death so carelessly?"

"I do what has to be done."

"You're full of contradictions," said Elijah.

"Maybe so."

"Want some advice?"

"Not particularly."

"That's what I thought. But you keep in mind that it's going to come down to you having to choose between protecting your daughter or your granddaughter--if you manage to stay alive that long."

"I have a plan."

"So you've said. You're an old man facing a bunch of cutthroats who, I might remind you, have your daughter's help. You up and steal their money and dope with little thought of what that could mean."

"I gave it some thought."

"Uh, huh."

"Well, let's call on your expertise, Elijah. What would you have done?"

Elijah put the bow down. He looked away from the fire. "Return what's theirs."

"And what about Spice. They want to use her in their dirty business."

"You could take her on a trip--someplace out of state."

"I could. I could also continue to hide like a mole. None of that would solve anything. The only solution is to put an end to the whole mess."

"The only way you're going to do that is call in the authorities and let Jo take what comes."

"I've thought about doing just that, but I can't. I think she's worth saving, if only for Spice's sake."

Elijah shook his head. "You'll end up dead."

Elmer re-lit his pipe.

Later, he dozed, sharing the edge of Spice's bed. He awoke frequently, hearing some strange or loud noise. Elijah moved about the camp, adding wood to the fire and stretching. Elmer was glad when daylight came.

The swamp morning arrived in increments, the night creatures retiring with a last blast and the morning ones bursting forth with great fanfare. Then, there were the beasts and serpents that wedged their awakening in between the noise makers.

They moved out early, as soon as it was light. Elijah led the way, saying he knew a shortcut.

"Through the quicksand patches?" asked Elmer.

"That's the way out."

The place looked treacherous. Streaks of fog hovered head-high over the bottoms like thin layers of smoke.

Underfoot, what appeared to be solid ground gave way quickly, forcing one to keep up a rapid walking pace. The land was continually changing. Dead trees, bleached skeletons of four-footed animals, and alligator skulls painted the desolate scene. Puddles of stagnated water stirred with insects and whatever else that survived beneath the green slime.

Strings of moss hung from the few live trees. Three vultures, their long necks bent, were perched on snags protruding from quicksand. Mosquitoes swarmed in droves.

Elmer stepped only in Elijah's tracks. The man carried Spice sitting on his shoulder. The sun whipped down in streams of oven-like waves. Elmer had never felt such heat.

The quicksand pools, some camouflaged by an overgrowth of thin grass, pockmarked the area. Elmer didn't know how Elijah knew where to step but hoped he'd not forgotten the route.

It was only after they had passed through the area that Elmer could breathe easier. He'd never been to this section of the swamp before. He hoped he'd never have to venture back into it. Down through the years strange tales had been told about the bottoms, about missing persons, and about strange lights.

Late in the evening they reached the edge of the swamp joining Elmer's land. Elijah put Spice down. "I'll leave you now to your own doings," he said.

"When I go back for the cases, will they be there?" said Elmer.

Elijah looked down at him. A slow smile broke his face. "If no one steals them, they should be."

Elmer grunted. He watched as Elijah disappeared through the brush. The man could move as quietly as a cat and when he desired, leaving no trail.

Leaving the swamp, they rested under the pines to wait for night. Under the protection of darkness, he and Spice crossed the field and approached the house from behind a barn.

They waited. Lights shone dimly through the windows. The red sports car, two pickup trucks, and a Mercedes were parked in the yard. He knew it was risky coming back, but there was no other way to carry out his plan.

He didn't know if the plan would work. It wasn't really a plan. It was only an idea which had a slim chance of working.

Two men walked out onto the front porch. They stood talking for several minutes. Later, both trucks cranked up and sped out of the yard.

He waited another thirty minutes, and they stole toward the rear of the house. He peeked in at the kitchen window.

Jo sat at the kitchen table. Gus Smith stood behind her, drinking a beer.

"Things are getting too complicated," said Janet Wolfe, entering the kitchen.

Chapter 20

Janet Wolfe poured a cup of coffee and sat across the table from Jo. She knew Gus's eyes were on her. This was no new experience for the woman. Men had always given her those looks. She knew how to dress to accentuate her good points, which, she often reminded herself, were many. The tight-fitting white slacks stretched to her form. The top two buttons of the pink blouse were left open, displaying what she considered a modest exposure of her fullness. She wore pink high-heels with straps.

Twisting her head, she flung hair over her shoulder. It was for Smith's benefit.

Janet never knew why she did those things. She didn't even know why she now got up and walked over to the sink, her movements exaggerated. It pleased her that Smith seemed to be locked in a trance.

She could hardly stand the man.

Janet was aware that Jo had paid particular attention to her performance. It delighted her to arouse jealousy in women.

When Rastus proposed to her, she warned him that she was expensive, that she wasn't a country girl satisfied with the limitations of hick-town existence. If she moved south, she had advised him, he would have to provide her with one of those colonial mansions so beautifully shown in movies.

Rastus had kept his word, to a point. He was just so, so reluctant to take chances. He wanted everything to be neat and precise. She had managed to change that. She had threatened to leave him and return to Michigan if he continued his miserly ways.

Janet considered Southerners beneath her. She thought the men were painfully macho and the women insufferably boring. Whenever she visited with her friends in Detroit, she lumped all Southerners into the "redneck" category, a people who chased around in pickup trucks with a pistol on the seat, a rifle hanging over the back window, and a six-pack on the floorboard. Janet had forgotten that many of her Michigan friends had Southern roots and had traveled frequently in the South. She never guessed that she bored them with her anti Southern tirade.

Some of her observations, one friend had advised, were probably accurate, but the chance of being run over by a big-wheeled pickup truck was probably no greater than getting raped in a Detroit park in broad daylight.

Jo said something, but Janet was concentrating on another walk to the sink. She stared back at Gus Smith. "Don't you have anything better to do than gaze at me?"

He grinned. "When a coon dog trees, I hear the music."

"Hillbilly!"

"And proud of it."

Jo hit the table with her fist. "This isn't getting us anyplace!"

Janet sat, crossing her legs. "Then what do you suggest we do? He's your father."

"Don't ask her," said Smith. "I'm the one who'll decide that."

"Then decide," Janet snapped back. "Find him!"

"We're looking!"

"By hanging around here drinking beer?"

Smith threw the empty can against the wall. "Don't be giving me orders! *I'm* the one who brought you two into this deal, remember? I'll get the money and stuff back."

"Sure. The old fool is going to walk in here and hand it all over plus the kid. You don't have the slightest idea where he's hiding."

"We'll find him. I got people searching right now."

"Those fools? They couldn't find their way to Savannah without a map!"

Jo lit a cigarette. "I want out when you get the cases back. I'm tired of my folks being treated like they are. I want this crap to end."

Smith turned to her. "What you talking about?"

"I'm talking about quitting," she said, drawing deeply on the cigarette. "I'm talking about getting out."

"You ain't quittin' nothing, baby. You're in this up to your ears."

"I'll show you. I'm through with it."

He slapped her hard across the face. She jerked back. He slapped her again, knocking her to the floor. "*You* ain't showing me nothing!"

Janet jumped up. "Stop that!" She cursed him. "You hit her again, and you'll have me to fight."

He grabbed her, pinning her arms down. She felt his body moving against hers. "You ain't half the hot mama you think you are. You fool with me, and I'll show you some real man stuff."

"Let me go!"

Jo struggled to her feet, wiping blood from her mouth. "Don't you ever hit me again," she told him. "If you do, I'll see you in prison, if it's the last thing I do. I mean it!"

Janet shoved him back. "You fool! Learn to control your temper, or you'll ruin everything."

"Yeah. So I'm sorry. Just stop pushing me, okay?" He snatched a can of beer from the refrigerator.

"Sit down," said Janet. "The both of you."

They sat at the table. She flipped her hair. "I don't know why I ever got mixed up with you two."

"I do," said Smith. "For the money."

"Well, I'm ready to make another trip, and you don't have the stuff. I didn't make the plunge for one lousy trip."

"Rastus was supposed to help us find the old man," said Smith. "He was supposed to get the kid for us, too. He ain't done nothing but talk."

"What did you expect?" said Janet. "You want him to search the swamp? He made it plain to you and your friends that he wasn't going to get directly involved with the details of the operation."

"Yeah, well, when I see him, I'm going to ask for some answers," said Smith. "With the money we're paying you, we--"

"Oh, shut up," said Jo. "You know he didn't promise to do anything specific."

"For a share of the profits we oughta be getting more out of them."

"Like what?" prompted Janet.

Smith grinned. "Some *real* kindness would do for starters."

"You're a pig," she snapped.

"I ain't gonna say what you are."

They stared at each other. Janet was beginning to regret becoming involved with them. At first it was a perfectly legal and proper act that Rastus was to perform--for a handsome fee. All he had to do was place a child in the hands of the rightful mother. It would be so simple. And it would have been if it had not been for the old man.

Rastus, having failed in his promise to deliver the kid to her mother (for a fee paid in advance), had wanted to discontinue any further transactions with the two. She shared his feelings until Smith offered her $10,000 to deliver a large package to a hotel in downtown Atlanta.

Of course, she knew what was in the package, but who would suspect a beautiful woman driving a Mercedes? Who could turn down so much money for such a simple task?

But Rastus was becoming worried. Suppose, he had suggested, the Feds knew about the hotel drop and had the place under surveillance. She had laughed it off. She could always claim that Gus had threatened her life. Who would believe him over her? He was an ex-con.

She smiled to herself. She had enjoyed her shopping spree in Atlanta. Then there was the money and cocaine Goodhand had stolen. Gus had promised them a share if they helped to recover it.

Janet Wolfe loved excitement. She was no longer bored with Rastus or Action. She loved money--large amounts of it. Why not deliver a few packages? Unlike Jo, she would never use the stuff herself. Only a fool did that. But Jo hadn't acted like she was on the stuff lately.

"Are you still using?" she asked Jo.

"I'm trying not to. It's hell."

"She's a scatter brain," offered Smith. "A little of the stuff never hurt nobody."

"It makes a fool out of you," said Janet.

"Keep on. One of these days you'll overload yourself, woman."

Jo poured coffee and lit a fresh cigarette. "How long we got to come up with the cargo, Gus?"

"I was supposed to deliver that batch to D. C. next week. They said I'd better have it or the old man."

"There you are," said Janet. "Your choice has been made for you."

"Meaning?" said Jo.

"Meaning just that. Those are not Boy Scouts you're dealing with, you know."

"No one is going to hurt my father or my daughter."

"Then I suggest you find him and talk to him," said Janet. "Or *you* might not live long enough to see either one again."

"I don't care about myself."

"Well, I care about me," said Smith. "I care a lot about my hide."

"Then get out and find Goodhand," said Janet.

"I already told you. I got people working on it!"

"It's your life."

Smith cursed her. "One of these days--"

Janet ignored the remark. She had been called worse. The money was uppermost in her mind. "Even if you find him, he might not lead you to the cases."

"Oh, but he will," said Smith. " All I got to do is get word to him that he brings me my property or he loses his daughter."

They both looked at him. "Hey, I didn't say I'd actually do you in, Jo, baby. What I'm saying is that all I need to do is make him think I will."

Janet saw the smile creep across the puffed face. She didn't like what she felt at that moment. "Well, it's a threat that might just work."

Smith chuckled, swallowing beer. "That old man will come running with my stuff once he gets the word."

"Yeah," said Janet, hip swinging to the stove for coffee. "All you have to do is get him word. Nothing to it."

He watched her walk back to the table, his eyes running over her. "You sure know how to walk, sweetheart."

Janet hoped she wasn't overdoing it. She had to be more careful. It was hard to break old habits. She smiled quickly at Jo. "Men are such little boys, aren't they?"

"And some women are such--well, you know what I mean."

Janet smiled tightly. "You should know."

"I didn't like you the first time I saw you," said Jo. "I must say, my first impression of you was not favorable. It still isn't."

Janet threw her head back. "I don't believe I ever had an impression concerning you. Perhaps it's because I knew so much about you before we met."

Smith laughed. "Go to it, ladies. Sic' em!"

Janet heard a car turn in at the driveway. "Who could that be?"

"I ain't expecting nobody," said Smith, pulling a nine-millimeter automatic pistol from his waistband. He hurried to the front of the house. "It's okay," he called. "It's just Spark and Sam."

The two men followed Smith into the kitchen. Spark's red hair curled out from a dingy cap. He grinned at Janet.

Sam Black, Janet saw, was smart enough to wear civilian clothes. She hated discussing criminal matters with a uniformed officer. It was too much like confessing.

Black fascinated Janet. His height and broad shoulders were such a contrast to Rastus's form. She went to the stove to refill her cup even though she really didn't want any more coffee. "How have you been, Sam?" she said, her voice soft.

"Fine. You?"

She tendered him a quick smile. "Guess?"

"Yeah. Everybody's up tight right now. But we'll find the stuff. The old man can't hide forever."

"True. But Gus doesn't have forever, does he?"

"Guess not."

"Look," said Spark, his thin face twisted in disapproval at the play between Sam and Janet. "Let's get down to business." He pulled a chair out from the table and sat down. "Get me a beer, Jo."

Jo glanced at him. "Get it yourself!"

"Let me," offered Janet. She brushed against Sam when setting the can before Spark. "You were saying, Spark."

"Here's how I got it figured. The old man and the young'n can't be hiding nowhere except in the swamp. We spotted a dark blue Dodge parked at Miss Mollie's. Sam here checked it out. It belongs to Goodhand. We questioned the old woman, but she claims she don't know a thing. Says she woke up one morning, and there was the car. Said she thought it belonged to some hunters."

"I'll get the truth out of her," said Smith.

"How?" Sam asked "By beating her?"

"Now, you look--"

"So what now?" Janet interrupted. "You going into the swamp to search for them?"

"That's exactly what I have in mind," said Spark. "Sam here can get a tracking bloodhound with no problem. We'll find them."

171

"Okay," said Smith, clapping his hands. "Get on it. If he ain't got my stuff with him, make him take you to where he's got it hid. Don't take any crap off him."

"Suppose he won't?" said Black. "You know how stubborn the old codger can be."

"Tell him if he wants to see his daughter alive, he'd better cooperate. If that doesn't work, well, he's got the brat with him. Use your imagination."

"I ain't going for none of that," Sam said. "Not hurting a kid."

"Hey, he won't know it's a bluff," said Smith. "Man, do I have to explain everything?"

"So long as we understand one another," said Sam.

Smith's face reddened. "I think you got my drift, Sam. I gave my word, didn't I? You get my stuff back, and I'll make it worth your time."

"All right. We'll start the dog out first thing in the morning."

"Bring them back here," said Smith. "I need to explain a few things to that man."

Janet stood. "I must be going. Can I drop you off someplace, Sam?"

"Sure."

Chapter 21

Elmer waited until Janet turned onto the highway before leading Spice around to the side of the house. Getting down on his knees and crawling under the porch, he pulled the squeaking access door open and helped Spice through and crawled inside. "Stay there until I turn on the light," he whispered.

He felt his way around the table, found the light, and switched it on. Quietly, he opened a can of fruit cocktail and poured it in a dish. He filled a glass with warm fruit juice and set it before Spice. "How about some pork and beans?"

"Okay."

Loud curses came from the kitchen. There are times when nothing ever goes right, he thought, looking down at the child he had raised from a baby. A man works and hopes that his decisions are the correct ones—then the world tries to drown him with its corruption. He wondered if there would ever be an end to it.

Elmer was relieved to hear the television come on in the den. There would be less chance of anyone hearing any accidental noise from the cellar.

Spice cleaned her plate and whispered that she was sleepy. He knew how tired she must be. The last few days had been a nightmare. He pulled a blanket over her for the fall night brought a chill to the cellar. She fell asleep almost immediately.

Elmer lay on his cot, his mind running over the events of the past few days. What would he do if Elijah had taken the briefcases? Without the cases he had no plan. There would be nothing with which to bait the trap.

He could not confide in anyone concerning Smith and his activities, not the lawyer who had conspired against him, or the local authorities. So, whatever action he took could involve no one. It would have to be his alone.

"You should have thought about using bloodhounds sooner," he heard Smith yell.

They would start the dog tracking at daylight. He didn't have much time. The dog would surely lead them to the cellar entrance under the porch.

Would they not also track to Elijah's cabin? What if the dog went sniffing at the hollow tree? Surely they would search the cavity, and if by the slimmest of chances the briefcases were still there, they would retrieve them.

Elmer didn't know what he should do, but one thing was certain. When morning came, he'd better have figured his next move. He remembered crossing three streams after leaving Elijah's cabin. Would that slow the dog?

There was one thing in his favor. They would have to cross the quicksand bottoms. That should delay them.

He awoke early. So did the intruders in the house. Apparently Spark had stayed the night, for he heard him call to Smith from the back porch. Elmer awoke Spice with a caution to keep quiet. He climbed the steps to listen at the door.

Jo entered the kitchen. Spark came in from outside. Elmer heard the clink of dishes and cabinet doors being closed, catching bits and pieces of their conversation, but nothing helpful to him.

Spark said he was leaving. Elmer heard the truck start up and drive off. It wasn't long before he heard the sports car speed down the drive.

He stayed at the door. The house remained quiet. Satisfied that everyone had left, he silently entered the closet. He cracked the door, peering into the hall.

They had a quick breakfast of cereal with diluted canned milk and jelly on toast. There was coffee left in the pot. He heated a cup in the microwave oven. It tasted weaker than he liked.

He still had no idea what he should do--only that they must get away. His car was at Miss Mollie's place, his truck at the car lot in town.

Careful to restore the kitchen as they had left it, he and Spice walked around the house three times, hoping to confuse the bloodhound and to keep them from finding the cellar door under the porch. They entered the woods below the cotton field.

Bill House ran the corn picker on the one hundred acres beyond the branch. He had turned at the end of the rows when Elmer and Spice approached.

"What's going on over at your place, Elmer?" asked the younger man. "I've been trying to call you for several days, and all I get is a lot of static from whoever answers the phone."

"Nothing for you to be concerned over, Bill. Some family problems. I need to borrow your truck."

"Help yourself. It's under the carport. Keys are in it."

"You know something, Poppy?" Spice said, when they were on the Interstate driving north.

"What?"

"I ain't had ice cream in a long time."

Elmer finished filling his pipe and struck a match. "I think I can remedy that."

"How?"

"Remember when I took you to see all those planes at the Air Force Museum at Warner Robins?"

"Yep?"

"What did we do afterwards?"

"We went to Ryan's, and you ate and ate."

"And I believe a certain little gal did, too."

She giggled. "I like ice cream."

"Well, Warner Robins is the next exit, and I bet Ryan's has some ice cream with your name on it."

"Poppy, they don't put names on ice cream."

"They don't?"

She shook her head. "Nope. It squirts out of a machine. Remember?"

"How about some food first? It's long past dinnertime."

"I want fried chicken."

"I don't know. Fried chicken is expensive."

She leaned back in the seat, thrusting her hands inside the bib of the overalls. "Poppy, you can charge it, can't you?"

"They don't know me there."

"Then tell them you're my poppy! Don't you know anything?"

"You think that'll solve the problem?"

"Yep."

"Okay, I think so, too."

Spice grinned. "Aren't you glad you got me?"

"Sometimes yes. Sometimes no."

She studied him through squinting eyes. "That doesn't sound like my poppy."

He puffed on the pipe, slowing down for the exit. "Why is that?"

"Just doesn't. My poppy is always glad he's got me 'cause I'm a smart little girl, aren't I?"

"Well, since you put it that way, I guess I'll have to admit you're pretty special."

A broad smile met his glance. "I knew that."

She unbuckled the seatbelt, snapped it back, and unbuckled it again. "Let's get chocolate ice cream."

"All right. Buckle up."

She fastened the belt.

Spice finished her meal with a dish stacked with chocolate ice cream. "We should have ice cream for breakfast, too," she said.

"Too much ice cream isn't good for you."

"Too much beans ain't, either."

He checked into a motel near I-75. Spice climbed onto one of the double beds. "Turn on the TV, Poppy."

He switched on the set to the public channel and leaned back in a chair, feeling unusually tired. Somehow, he had to end it. He didn't know how much longer he could run and hide. He had to put things in order before it was too late.

The dog might or might not trail them back to the house, depending on how well it could track and how scent lasted in the humidity of the swamp. He hoped that the dog failed. The cellar was their last hiding place.

He'd wait a couple of days. Maybe by then Smith would have left to make another haul from Florida.

For two days he and Spice ate, rested, and napped away the time. He returned to Action at night and drove by the farm. He saw no vehicles parked in the yard. The house appeared dark.

He drove out to Rastas Wolfe's restored mansion and saw the Lincoln and Mercedes parked in the carriage house. Elmer slipped the .45 in his waistband and buttoned the jacket.

Janet Wolfe came to the door. "Of all people! Do come in."

"Is Rastus around?"

"In his study." She led the way upstairs. The lawyer greeted them cordially. "Where you been, Elmer? I've been worried about you two."

"Hate to disturb you like this, Rastus."

"Forget that. Sit down."

The lawyer sat behind his desk. He glanced at his wife. "We've been worried about you, Elmer--you and the kid."

"Well, I did it," said Elmer. "It might have been the worst thing to do but didn't see as how I had any choice left."

"You did what?" said Rastus.

Elmer concentrated on filling his pipe. "I spent most of the afternoon in the U.S. Attorney's office in Macon."

"You *what?*"

"I told them about Gus Smith and his dope-trafficking activities, about how they were using my place, and about his hauls out of Miami to Atlanta and D.C."

Rastus leaned forward. "What about Jo's part in it? Did you tell them about her, too?"

"I told them everything. I named Spark, the deputy Sam Black, and all the others I'd seen out at the farm with that bunch."

"You sent your daughter to prison, Elmer."

"Maybe not. I think she's being coerced, and I told them that."

"You signed a statement concerning all that?"

Elmer nodded.

Rastus muttered under his breath.

"The Attorney said he was going to direct an immediate investigation. Said Action might already be part of an undercover operation."

"I sure wish you had consulted me first. I think you acted prematurely."

"I'm desperate, Rastus. Those people are giving me a bad time."

The lawyer stood. "Where you going now?"

"I have some friends in the next county. Probably spend a few days there. It shouldn't take the Feds long to do whatever it is they do in narcotic cases."

Elmer got to his feet. "Come on, Spice. We'd better get moving."

He looked at Janet. She smiled tightly. "You ever get started on that story you mentioned?"

She shook her head. "I really haven't given it much thought."

"Well, maybe we'll all have more time on our hands when this mess is finished."

He started out. The lawyer followed him and Spice down the curving stairway. "I heard rumors you might have some property belonging to Smith," Rastus said casually. "I hope there's nothing to it."

Elmer paused at the door. "If I did, the U.S. Attorney's office would want it as evidence, wouldn't they?"

Rastus nodded. "In all likelihood."

He put Spice in the truck and drove off. He turned onto the highway, going slowly, lights off. Shortly, he saw the Mercedes pull out of the driveway and speed down the road.

He returned the truck. Bill House advised he'd seen nothing of dogs or men in the area. "I've been working over near your house the last couple of days, Elmer. No one was around while I was there."

They crossed through the woods and around a field. He saw no vehicles or lights. Since he could not know if the dog had trailed them to the house or if they discovered the cellar, he decided the loft of the barn would offer the best hiding place for now.

Elmer helped Spice up the ladder into the hayloft. He sat near the door at the front where he could see the house, wondering how fast Janet Wolfe would spread the word.

"Poppy, did we do all those things you told that man?"

"What things?"

"The things about Macon. You know, that attorney stuff."

"No."

"Poppy, you told a big one, didn't you?"

"Will you forgive me?"

"Yep,"

An hour later, two pickup trucks and a Mercedes pulled into the yard.

Chapter 22

"I'm gonna kill him!" Gus Smith shouted, slamming his fist to the kitchen table. "First, he hides the kid, and then he steals from me, and now he's run mouthing to the Feds. I'm gonna kill him!"

Jo took beer from the refrigerator. She was afraid to argue or plead with Gus when he was so angry. Anyway, she'd decided that her father would not be easy to find. She placed the beer on the table. Janet Wolfe opened a can, taking a long drink. Deputy Sam Black, in uniform, sat across the table from her; Spark and Jim Lee appeared fascinated by Janet's low-cut red blouse. They momentarily ignored the beer.

Jo watched as Janet practiced her craft, ever the teasing temptress. She wore black shorts, tight to a fault. Janet left the table and walked back and forth. Jo thought she overdid it.

"The old man might be pulling a bluff," said Janet.

"If that's true, then he knows you are involved," informed Jo, lighting a cigarette.

"There's no way he could have proof of that," said Janet. "He knows nothing, and I'm not involved!"

"You're involved," said Black. "You made a delivery to Atlanta, remember?"

"Yes, but I didn't know what was in the package. I still don't. I had to go to Atlanta anyway. I was just doing Gus a favor."

"Yeah," said Spark. "For ten thousand. Some favor!"

"Did you hear something?" Gus said suddenly, cocking his head.

"Hear what?"

"It was a noise outside, out back. Check it out, Spark. Might be the old man snooping around."

"Come on, Jim Lee," ordered Spark, pulling a snub-nose .38 from his jacket pocket.

"My father is somewhere in another county," informed Jo. "You don't think he's fool enough to come near this place, do you?"

"What he says he's going to do and what he does is two different things," retorted Janet, pushing hair from over her face.

"I know I heard something," insisted Smith, peering out through the screen door.

"It couldn't be the Narcs, could it?" Jo asked anxiously. "They wouldn't have had time to start a stakeout, would they?"

"Shut up!" ordered Smith. "I'm trying to listen."

Jo believed Gus was hearing things. Besides, she didn't believe her father would go to the law. He had to know that she was as deeply involved as Gus and felt he would go to almost any length to keep her from going back to prison. Still, she couldn't be absolutely certain. Spice came first with him. He must be getting fed up with them and the trouble they were causing. Did she really know her father? How long would he try to protect her?

She had to be a terrible disappointment to him. She had been a failure and was sick of it all. What she thought would be exciting had somehow become tiresome. Most of the time Gus was unbearable. The more money he made, the more he wanted. What was supposed to have been a short-term operation had turned into full-time employment She wished they could recover the money and cocaine her father had taken, settle loose ends, and quit before it was too late.

Spark and Jim Lee returned. "Nothing out there," announced Spark.

"Let's decide what to do," Janet said impatiently, sitting down.

"What's for us to decide?" said Black. "I ain't done nothing the cops would be interested in."

"Me, neither," said Spark. "All I've done is tried to find the old man. I mean, he's missing ain't he? I was just being a good citizen."

Gus chuckled. "What did I tell y'all in the beginning? I told you I wasn't asking nobody to break the law. Everybody's clean except me, Jo, and Janet there."

"Don't you include me as one of your partners!" shouted Janet, jumping up. "I didn't know and still don't know what was in that package."

"She's right," Jo said. "Gus didn't tell her. I didn't, either."

Janet spread her hands. "See. I have nothing to worry about."

The deputy opened a second beer. "Gus, I hope you weren't serious about killing anybody. You do a hit, and every cop, crooked or not, will be on your trail."

"You running my business now?"

Jo never knew when Gus was serious. He'd given her his word that no harm would come to her father. She had to believe him. She refused to think otherwise.

"I think the old man is running a bluff, hoping to scare you off," said Black. "Somehow, he's made the connection between Gus and Janet. He probably thinks that Gus and Jo will skip the state and leave him with all that money."

"Yeah," said Spark. "He's a smart one. We all run, and he ends up with a fortune."

"I'm gonna get my property," Smith said.

"How?" Janet wanted to know. "You can't even find him. How are you going to make him come to you?"

"I got ways."

"The dog sure was no help," said Spark.

"I still say somebody is in that swamp and helped the old man and the kid," Black said. "Somebody dragged dead skunks all over the place. The dog stayed confused."

"It had to be that swamp giant," said Jim Lee, swallowing beer. "I ain't going back in there!"

Thunder pounded in the southwest. Lightning flashed along the horizon. A gust of wind whipped through. A barn door slammed.

"Sounds like a storm coming up," said Jo.

"And somebody might be at one of the barns," cautioned Smith. "Spark?"

"You're sure jumpy, Gus. Didn't you just hear the wind push against the house?"

"Go take a look!"

Mumbling, Spark started out. Lightning streaked to the ground nearby. Rain broke loose. Spark returned to his chair. "I'm scared of lightning."

"Ain't nothing out there," said Black. "Not even that swamp giant would be hanging around in this weather."

Smith shook his head. "You people are something else."

"This is getting us nowhere," said Janet. "I want to know what you plan to do."

Smith opened a can of beer. He looked at Jo. "What do you think, babe? You believe your old man tried pulling a bluff or what?"

She lit a cigarette. She wanted to give the right answer. "I've never known him to play games. We must assume he did what he said."

Smith appeared to be thinking. "So, what should we do now?" he directed at her.

Lightning flashed overhead. Rain pounded the roof. Jo drew on the cigarette. "I think we should cut the operation. Maybe leave the state until we know for sure whether he informed on us."

"What do we do about the money and coke he stole?"

"I think I can get it back. In a couple of weeks I'll come back here alone and talk to him. I'm sure he'll turn it over to me if he thinks he's done with us."

Smith slapped her. "Yeah, you'd come back. You'd get it all, and that'd be the last I'd see of you!"

Jo left the table. Standing near the door, she looked out into the wet night. She wanted to kill him. Spark and the deputy exchanged glances. Sam Black thought he read Spark's thoughts. If they were ever to get their hands on the money and the cocaine in Elmer Goodhand's possession, no better plan presented itself than Jo's. All they had to do was wait until she returned in a few weeks, alone, and talk the old man into giving her the briefcases. Black thought of several ways he and Spark could get the stash without Jo or Smith's knowledge.

"That's the best idea I've heard all night," said Black. "It's sure to work, Gus."

"I don't know. There's too much at stake."

It was Spark's turn. "The way I see it, you ain't got no cause to suspect Jo. She's been right there with you all along, even against her own pa and young'un. It don't make much of a nohow that you don't trust the rest of us, but Jo?"

"I like her idea," said Janet. "It doesn't look like you have a choice, Gus. The old man certainly isn't going to deal with you."

Jo sipped beer. "I could leave dad a note explaining everything. Tell him we'd leave him and Spice alone if he returned the cases."

The deputy was tired of working for low pay. One day he hoped to be the sheriff, but that was not in the immediate future. Getting half of everything the old man had taken from Smith would allow him to bide his time. If he had found the briefcases, no one, not even Spark, would have known. Why share a fortune if you don't have to? Glancing at Janet, he returned the quick smile, reading her like a map. She, too, was thinking of ways to get her hands on the wealth. He wondered how far she would go. She was a woman who went after what she wanted. She had called the meeting on the pretense of believing Goodhand's story. He didn't think she fell for it anymore than he did. The old man wasn't the kind to throw his daughter to the wolves.

He studied her, wondering about her motives. What did she need with so much money? Wasn't Rastus providing her with the good life?

Janet, he suspected, needed to be fed a constant flow of adventure and money.

The deputy had never been involved with drugs or people like Gus Smith before. His record with the department was clean, but the deal Smith offered involved too much money to turn down, especially considering how little he had to do to earn it. Five hundred a week just to keep an eye on things and pass along any information he picked up could hardly be called work. Since going on Smith's payroll, he'd been on the lookout for other connections where the big money flowed. Unfortunately, a town Action's size presented few opportunities.

Things would be different if only he and Spark had found the briefcases first. Where was Smith hiding his money now? One thing was for certain; he wasn't hauling it around in his car. Maybe he and Spark should do another search when they left. "If I were you, Gus, I'd drive on up to Atlanta with Jo, make this last delivery, and take off for a couple weeks like Jo said."

Gus Smith studied the faces at the table. He glanced at Jo standing at the door. He appeared to be considering their suggestions. It was little enough Black had done to earn the money he was paying him. He couldn't even get a bloodhound to follow a fresh trail, coming up with a cockeyed story about somebody dragging skunks around. Did they take him for a fool?

They were idiots if they thought he was going to leave the state without settling with the old man. Jo's plan sounded like a play for a double-cross. Goodhand had been a problem from the beginning. Things would have worked smoothly if he had been out of the picture. With the kid along, he and Jo could have made twice the number of trips and felt safe doing it.

Well, the old man had been given more chances than he deserved. He was through playing with him. Nobody could steal from him and not pay the consequences. As soon as he recovered the cases, he was going to teach him what it meant to fool with Gus Smith.

Elmer Goodhand had to die.

He had to die in the swamp where the body would disappear. No one would ever know he killed him. If the brat was with him--well, she wouldn't be the first kid to become a victim of the swamp.

Chapter 23

The storm passed over by morning. Elmer watched from the barn loft as Smith and Jo put suitcases in the sports car and drive off. He waited until the sound of the car faded and climbed down from the loft.

"Poppy, I'm tired of sleeping in holes and barns," said Spice, following close behind. "I want my room back."

"Be patient, gal."

"How come you always say that, Poppy? How can I be patient when I don't know what patient is?"

He grunted.

"That sounds like you don't want to talk about it."

"How do you wake up so ready to do battle?"

"Is that what I do?"

"Yeah. Reminds me of your grandma."

She followed him into the house. "When do we eat?"

He went into the den to use the telephone. He called the car dealer where his truck was parked and asked that it be delivered to his house as soon as possible.

"Poppy, when do we eat?"

"We'll get something on the road."

The truck arrived an hour later. He drove to the Interstate and headed north. Exiting at the next town, they had breakfast at a fast-food restaurant and filled the gas tank.

He reached Luke McAllister's farm at noon. He found his old friend in the building housing poisonous snakes. Elmer waited until Luke had complained about the weather, the sour disposition of diamondbacks, and the low prices paid for serum.

"I need four rattlers," said Elmer, "with the rattling part cut off."

Luke studied him. "You want me to cut off the rattlers?"

Elmer nodded.

"I take it you want really potent snakes?"

Elmer nodded again.

"You know that it ain't always the size that determines the amount of venom, don't you?"

"No, I didn't."

"Sometimes the younger ones deliver more venom per strike."

"You're the snake doctor."

"I don't think I want to know what you have in mind, do I?"

Elmer said nothing.

"That's what I thought," said Luke. "Well, I can fix you up, but boy you'd better be careful handling them."

"Make it as safe as you can for me."

"Elmer, you can't put a muzzle on these things like you can a dog, you know. There's no way I can make it safe."

"Can you put two in one container and two in another?"

"I can do that. What kind of container you thinking about?"

"I don't know. How do you transfer them?"

"In a garbage can mostly. Sometimes I use a burlap sack."

"Sacks will better suit my purpose," said Elmer. "I'll be transferring them later."

"And that's where it can get tricky," warned Luke. "You'd be surprised how quickly a rattler moves. If he's in a sack, it can be darn risky."

"Suppose I wanted to transfer two from a sack to a suitcase?"

"Well, supposing that, I'd place the sack inside the suitcase, carefully making sure the open end of the sack faced away from me," said Luke, emphasizing with slow hand motions. "Then I'd gently pull a bit of the bottom of the sack to the outside of the suitcase, keeping in mind, of course, that you've already got the suitcase closed to a small crack--leaving just enough opening to slip and slide the sack out. That should force the snakes out of the sack and into the case."

"Sounds easy enough."

"Uh, huh. Easy, you say. Well, old friend, just a little old slip could send you to the promised land on the next shuttle."

"I'll be careful."

"You do that, Elmer. Now, walking around with a bag of these fellows in each hand ain't no snap, either. Don't be letting the sack bump against your legs."

"How do I carry the sack?"

"I'm going to fix that. We'll use a piece of rope to tie the sack and serve as a handle."

The diamondbacks Luke selected were under four feet. They appeared big in diameter to Elmer and seemed to be ill-tempered. He maintained a safe distance while Luke held one behind its head and cut off the rattlers. He dabbed a thick salve to the wound.

"How much air will they need if they're in a tight box?" Elmer asked.

"Not much. Punch several holes in it with a knife. Of course, it could depend on how long you plan to keep 'em."

"No longer than necessary."

"Somehow, I'm relieved to hear that. As I remember, you used to have a horror of snakes."

"I still do."

"Then you remember this. A bite from one of these will likely kill you unless you get treatment pretty quick."

He paused in tying a sack with rope. "But that's the whole idea, ain't it?"

Elmer said nothing, giving his attention to filling his pipe.

Luke placed the two sacks of dangerous cargo in a metal garbage can and tied down the lid. He secured the can in the back of the truck. "Let's hope nobody steals your truck or the can."

"What's in the can?" Spice asked when they drove off.

"Something very dangerous, so don't go near that can. Don't even climb up on the truck, understand?"

"Okay."

Elmer decided he wouldn't risk driving on the Interstate. He stayed on secondary roads, keeping his speed down. Spice curled up on the seat, resting her head on his leg. The day turned hot, and he switched on the air condition. She dozed off.

He could not be certain his plan would work. The briefcases might be gone. Elijah probably saw him place the cases in the tree. All his planning would be for nothing if the stuff were gone, but it might be for naught, anyway. He would only get one chance and wouldn't even think about what might happen to Spice if they killed him.

What chance in life would she have, left to Jo's instability and whims?

He had to succeed with his plan.

But one slip would be the end of him.

Regardless of what happened in life, one could always find a reason for living, he'd decided. There was always something up ahead you could look forward to, if only the sunrise. Children could be the real sunshine or the storm. Either way they could test the wisdom of a Solomon.

When Lucy died, he was left with a void. Even his work and books proved inadequate to fill the emptiness. Then Spice was dumped on him, and the little millstone turned out to be something that brightened his days. Sometimes end-on-end--

But there was her future to think about. It called for deliberate planning. The solution seemed simple. He'd place her with a good family. He had not discarded the idea completely. If only he could be sure that she would be loved and well-cared for, but how could you be certain about such things? There was so much deceit and cruelty in the world you could never really trust anyone.

He just didn't know what he should do. It was no easier being a grandparent than it was being a parent. He'd hate to think he failed at both.

He reached Action after dark and drove out to the House farm. Bill's wife, Ellie, a short plump woman, had no children and never wanted any. She was short-spoken, and her high-pitched voice could be grating. The woman was about the most no-nonsense person Elmer had ever met. Ellie said what she meant, and meant what she said. Everything in her house had to be immaculate, including her husband. She accepted no excuses. Ellie agreed immediately--and with what Elmer thought was a hint of delight--to keep Spice for a few days.

"Spice is one young'un I can always get along with," she said.

"I don't want to stay with her," Spice whispered to Elmer.

"You do, too," squealed Ellie. "Now into the house with you. I'm baking a chocolate cake, and there's ice cream just crying to be eaten."

"Oh, all right," said Spice. "I guess if you've got all that, I can stay a little while. Bye, bye, Poppy. Don't forget where you left me."

He parked the truck behind the house. He believed Smith and Jo had gone to Florida. If Smith followed his usual routine, they would return to the farm in two days and wait for the call from Atlanta. That didn't give him much time.

He retrieved the twelve-gauge pump shotgun from the study closet and loaded it with double-ought buckshot. Filling the loops of a belt with shotgun shells, he found the holster for the .45 pistol and attached it to the belt.

He must have everything ready when the time came, for he'd have to move fast. He wrote Jo a note and placed it on the table where they would be sure to see it.

Carrying the shotgun, belt, flashlight, and canteen out to the truck, he drove down to the pond and parked the truck where it could be seen from the house.

Returning to the house on foot, he prepared the only food he would take--peanut butter between crackers. He put these in a plastic bag with an extra pouch of pipe tobacco and matches.

While cleaning the pistol, he mentally went over his list, hoping to remember everything. Satisfied, he poured a cup of coffee, switched off all the lights, and went out onto the porch. A breeze brought a chill to the night. Down at the pond, frogs croaked a message of contentment. Cicadas vibrated chatter from the trees. He remembered that he would need a blanket and went inside to search a closet. He found the old army blanket and folded it tightly, securing it with a belt. Returning to the porch, he wondered what else might have slipped his mind.

A pickup slowed going past the house. Elmer withdrew the .45 from his belt and placed it on the table next to his chair. The pickup turned around and drove slowly by again. He sipped coffee and smoked the pipe. Whoever was in the truck must have decided no one was at the house. Elmer relaxed, feeling better now that he was finally doing something.

He wished there were another way. There wasn't, not if he was to keep Jo out of prison.

From far in the swamp came the sound of killer dogs roaming on a hunt. Elmer suddenly felt cold, and he hated having to go back in there. Would he live to come out? Reaching for coffee, his hands shook.

Chapter 24

Elmer left the house at dawn and hurried to the truck parked near the pond, feeling tired after staying awake all night watching the road. A layer of dense fog hung over the swamp. Untying the lid of the garbage can, he slowly removed it and carefully lifted the two sacks of rattlers. He placed them at the rear of the truck and climbed down, pausing to catch his breath.

The old man hung the shotgun over his shoulder by the strap, buckled on the ammunition belt with the holstered pistol, and secured the canteen and blanket over his other shoulder. He was glad the morning was cool and hoped to be deep into the swamp before the day turned hot.

How much time did he have? He could only speculate when Smith and Jo would return but hoped they wouldn't get back until later in the day. Otherwise, he might not have time to properly set the trap. It was crucial to have everything in readiness before Smith found him.

He lifted the sacks off the truck and limped toward the thick growth beyond the dam.

Stooping, he pressed through a curtain of vines, believing he heard a vehicle slow down on the highway. Did it turn in at his driveway? Suppose it was Spark or the deputy? They would surely see the note. If they knew the location of Snake Island, they might try to beat Smith to the money and cocaine. Had he put himself in a no-win situation?

Elmer tried to pick up his pace.

He'd only gone a short distance before having to stop to rest. Sweat ran off his face. He used a sleeve. The sacks were heavy, and the ropes cut into his hands. He wished he'd worn gloves.

The old man pushed on, working his way through a thick shield of bamboo vines, feeling the sharp prick of the thorns against his body. A snake in one of the sacks twisted violently. A thorn had stuck him.

The fog began to lift, hanging in strips to form a ceiling below the treetops. Elmer reached a small clearing and put the sacks on the ground. He had to rest. "Only a minute," he told himself. "I'll just rest for a minute."

A wild boar, the bristles along his back sticking up like stiff pieces of wire, rooted along a nearby stream. The tusks, curving crookedly from his jaws, could rip a man's thigh to the bone. Elmer watched him closely and so did a large moccasin with his head raised a foot off the ground.

The boar spied the snake at that same moment and leaped to the kill. The serpent struck the hog on the shoulder. A snakebite to a hog is not much more than a pin prick--and not fatal.

Jaws clamped down on the snake. The hog shook the twisting mass violently while the withering creature had no defense. The boar devoured him.

The snake-eater sniffed and searched the ground to find a morsel he might have missed. Head raised and ears cocked, the hog saw Elmer who slipped the shotgun from his shoulder and released the safety.

They stared at each other. Eventually, the boar turned, wandering off through a thicket of briars and berry bushes.

Elmer picked up the sacks and crossed the stream. A dog howled from afar.

He came upon the partially eaten carcass of a buck the swamp dogs had killed. A pair of lanky vultures clumsily struggled to become airborne. Green flies paid him no attention.

A mockingbird perched high on a dead limb offered a repertoire of imitations. Dog days had passed, and the birds were singing again.

Elmer found the footing here uncertain. Recent rains had turned the ground to mud, and he slipped, almost falling on the sack of snakes. He picked himself up, raked off mud, and struggled on, breathing hard. His wet clothes held to him.

Leaving the stretch of mud, he put down the sacks and massaged his tired, aching hands, rubbed raw by the ropes. He gulped water from the canteen and found a place to sit. He had to rest. His arms trembled from the strain of holding the load away from his body.

Crows argued from the tops of dead trees. Mosquitoes gathered in, swarming to feed. Elmer filled his pipe and puffed a screen of smoke to discourage the pests.

Later, some rested, he picked up his cargo and slowly plodded through the jungle. It was a familiar knoll where he stopped to eat crackers. The sun showered directly from above. The heat and humidity drained him. He listened, in case man or beast was following him.

From the knoll, he turned eastward. Having no desire to venture toward the bottoms, he selected the longer route. Upon reaching the area where the tall, sharp-blade grass grew, he rested ten minutes before starting across, turning sideways in places as he was not able to hold the sacks above the grass alongside the deer trail. It was a teeth-grinding task. Pain vibrated through his aching muscles. The rope around his left hand broke the skin, drawing blood. He tied a handkerchief around the hand and pressed on.

Up ahead, an old alligator plowed through the grass and eased into a deep pool, hoping to snare the doe drinking at the edge nearby. Leaving the grass, Elmer sought the thick shade of a towering oak. Muscadine grapes hung from vines laced on a nearby hickory. Picking his footing, Elmer reached the vines and filled himself with the juicy fruit.

Reluctantly, he left the spot, for it was the only place he'd felt a breeze since early morning. An hour later, he entered a foreboding place where everything portrayed dying or death. The fissured crust felt rock-hard under his feet. Most of the trees stood in varying stages of decay, their limbs' stubby fingers groping outwardly. A heavy stench pervaded the air. Black buzzards, some circling high, some low, some parked on bare limbs, played their waiting game.

The man couldn't remember if he'd ever been in this part of the swamp before. He wondered if a freak in the mineral contents of the earth had caused the vegetation to die. The bleached bones of small and large animals lay scattered around a pool of green water.

He stopped abruptly. It dawned on him that there were no sounds. He had heard nothing but the scraping of his feet over the hard ground. No birds sang, and no insects conversed.

Elmer stood immobile, hearing nothing except his own breathing.

Wiping his face, he tried to hurry from the place.

He felt relieved once he left the desolation behind him and refused to even look back. A tall growth of cypress stretched ahead. He circled the patch of water-bound trees, looking for higher ground.

A breeze stirred. Elmer paused under an oak to rest. If he'd had the time he would have delayed longer, but time was rapidly slipping away. He should have already reached the hollow tree. Where had the time gone? The sun dropped low in the west.

Picking up the sacks, he labored on, lifting his feet as if they were weighted. Dogs howled from scattered locations to the north. It could signal the forming of a pack. Elmer shivered. He worried that his strength would play out before reaching the tree. Each step became a struggle. His boots weighed as if lead. The sacks frequently brushed against his legs. Sometimes he wasn't even aware of the danger. He ignored the sweat running into his eyes. Only one goal existed--find the oak!

He must reach the tree soon. Tomorrow, Smith would surely come. Others might already be close behind. A dog howled up ahead.

Where was the tree?

Blood trickled down the rope. The snakes twisted. The sack bounced against his leg. He lifted his feet. They felt so heavy.

"Poppy, don't you know nothing? That woman can't be my mother! I don't need a mother. I've got my Poppy. Don't you know that?"

The shadows lengthened, reaching for darkness.

"I bet you're teasing me, Poppy. Not all the stores run out of ice cream the same day!"

A bobcat screamed somewhere behind him. Or, was that a panther? He couldn't hold the snakes away from him any longer. The strength was gone from his arms.

"What do I want to be when I grow up? I want to be everything, Poppy. I want to be just like you."

He struggled for breath. How much farther?

"Little people aren't supposed to eat beans; don't you know that?"

He stopped, looking around. Where was the tree? Was this the place? Nothing about it looked familiar. Was he lost?

I must rest, he told himself. I'm not thinking straight. How far away are the dogs? Sounds like a large pack. No, those are coyotes. But he'd heard dogs, too. Or had he? Yes, but that was sometime ago. No, that's a dog. He knew a hound's howl when he heard it. But it was only one dog, wasn't it? Why are you getting upset over one mutt?

Must go on. Time is precious. Everything has to be in place--everything--

"By, By, Poppy. Don't forget where you left me."

The ropes tugged at his raw hands. Could snakes smell blood? Would they strike at the scent? His feet were so heavy--heavy--*"Tell you what, Poppy. I'll bet you a whole dollar I can eat a big dish of strawberries in sugar--hear me, Poppy? See, I've got a dollar in my pocket."*

No, I'm in the wrong place, he thought. The old oak is over there to my right. It can't be too far now. Why is it getting so dark so soon? I'll never find the tree in the dark. Tomorrow might be too late.

"I never had a mother. I don't want one. That woman can't be my mother. You're mistaken, Poppy. This little person doesn't need any mother. I've got my poppy. That's all I want."

Is that the tree? It looks like it. The sacks bumped against his legs. His arms throbbed with pain. His shoulders and back cried for relief.

An owl hooted. The shadows surrendered to the twilight. The wet clothes felt cold against his body. He paused to swallow a drink of water.

Lifting the sacks of burden, he shuffled through vines. His bad leg turned numb. The pain subsided. The owl hooted again, sounding closer. He looked up. The large oak spread its limbs over the clearing like a protective hen covering her chicks.

He'd found the hollow tree! He stumbled, releasing his hold on the sacks as he fell. The sacks came alive, bulging with their angry contents.

Struggling to his feet, dizziness swept over him. He steadied himself, taking long, deep breaths. He trudged to the trunk of the tree, trying to massage out the soreness crippling his bleeding hands. Dogs howled in a pack over in the direction of Snake Island.

Elmer leaned against the oak, feeling chilled. Wind rustled through the trees. He untied the blanket and pulled it around him. Finding a stick, he probed the hollow of the tree.

The briefcases were gone!

Chapter 25

He searched the hollow of the large oak with his hand, grabbing, scratching. It was no use. The cases were not there. *Gone!*

He slumped to the ground, resting his back against the trunk. Closing his eyes, he tried to think. What was he going to do? Only one person could have taken the cases. Elijah must have followed him and secretly watched as he shoved them in the hollow of the tree. He'd gone back and taken them!

Or had he? The bloodhound could have led Spark and Sam Black to the oak. They would certainly not have told anyone they'd found the cache. Darkness settled thickly in the swamp. Autumn chill came on a teasing wind. Using the flashlight, he gathered dead limbs, cleaned off a place under the oak, and built a small fire.

The dogs howled a call for gathering. Crickets and locust began tuning in earnest. Water in an isolated pool splashed with sudden disturbance. A raccoon wandered into the spread light of the fire, sniffed the air, and then chased off.

Elmer munched crackers. His mind failed to function. Indecision engulfed him. He could neither turn back nor go on. Even now his time might have run out. Struggling to his feet, the old man gathered more wood for the fire.

He must keep the flame small, not knowing who might be searching for him or how close they were.

Hearing what might be a bear sneaking through thick growth, he held the shotgun ready, being in no mood to tolerate abuse from man or animal. He would not have been surprised if Smith or Spark appeared in his camp. Darkness would not stall them when there was a chance to recover the money and cocaine.

Elmer felt defeated, drained of all energy and hope. All his efforts had been wasted. Nothing had been done to ensure Spice's well-being. The warmth of the fire caressed his body, causing him to nod. He put a thicker limb on the fire, hoping that if he did fall asleep the flame wouldn't die out.

"Poppy, I'm tired of being little. Am I eating enough?"

What was that? How long had he been asleep? What could be making such a sound?

"Let's bake a cake, Poppy. We can do anything."

He jerked fully awake when a cat growled nearby. His head felt so heavy--

"Are you sure you mailed my letter to Santa Claus? I think he left me another kid's stuff! And he didn't bring you anything! I think he's getting too old for the job, don't you, Poppy?"

Who was that? Was someone standing over there? Where's my shotgun?

Elmer blinked as he stared across the ashes of a dead fire. Streaks of sunlight danced through the branches. He rubbed his eyes, knowing his mind was tricking him. The two briefcases were near the tree. He lifted them and then clapped his hands, wincing from the sudden pain. So Elijah wasn't a thief after all!

Wishing for a cup of coffee, he quickly ate cracker sandwiches and washed it down with water. Carrying the cases to the oak and opening them, he found little room in either one. Elmer removed the bags of cocaine and threw them into the cavity of the oak. From the other case, he took out the bundles of bills and shoved them in with the drugs.

Now came the ticklish part. Carefully, slowly, he untied a sack and gently placed it in a case. Reluctantly, using thumb and forefinger, he took hold of the bottom; while holding the burlap closed at the top, he shifted the dreaded weight toward the center of the sack.

It was a painstakingly slow process. Perspiration poured off his forehead in the early morning chill. Finally, with the snakes positioned where he wanted them, he pulled the bottom of the bag to the outside of the case while holding the lid down and began working the burlap out.

He wanted to just snatch the sack out and hope for the best, but he was dealing with creatures that could strike within the blink of an eye. It was not a time to hurry!

Elmer kept at it, tugging and pulling, working the sack farther and farther out through the narrow gap between the lid and the case. He hoped the chilly air would slow the snakes' reactions.

With stiff, aching hands, he wiped the water off his face. It was taking too long. He must do it quicker. Finally, after what seemed a stretched eternity, the burlap slid free. The odor made him wretch. Snapping the case closed, he latched it and limped away, gulping deep breaths of fresh air.

Wiping a handkerchief over his face, he soon returned to his work. His hands shook from the strain. Elmer followed the same procedure now, slowly, deliberately shifting the reptiles within the sack. When he released his hold on the top of the sack, a diamondback slithered out, seeming to jump toward the light. Elmer slammed the lid closed, pinching blood from his thumb in the process.

He held the lid down tightly, took a deep breath, and went back to work. It was taking too much time, but it couldn't be helped. The snakes searched for a way out, their heads near the small opening with tongues forking for direction.

Slowly, he tugged and worked the sack to the outside, inch by aching inch. He turned his head from the odor, breathing deeply. Sweat burned his eyes, and he rubbed them with the wet sleeves of his shirt.

Elmer hated snakes. He had always feared them, considering every species of the serpent a curse on mankind. Finally accomplishing the task, he secured the case and hurriedly prepared to move on. It would be a long trip through some of the thickest parts of the swamp. He must remember to conserve his strength whenever possible.

Having comfortable handles to hold onto now, he didn't have to worry about the snakes biting him through burlap.

Forcing himself to pause for a brief rest, he had to consider that Smith might already be at Snake Island. What if they were all there? What would he do then? If they saw or heard him, they would track him down and kill him. Someone might even now be waiting to shoot him on sight. Elmer didn't even know if his crazy idea would work. Maybe it was a fool thing to even attempt what he was doing.. He put the cases down and wiped his face. A doe leaped through the brush. Two large dogs chased close at her heels. His arms felt as if being pulled from their sockets as he lifted the cases. He circled a thick patch of bamboo vines, then turned westward. The way appeared treacherous, with thick brush and tall grass. A large deer bulldozed his way through the brush, startling Elmer so that he dropped both cases.

Passing through the thicket, Elmer gained better ground for walking and hoped to make up some lost time, but his body had little energy. Approaching Snake Island by mid-afternoon and pausing at the stream to listen, he waded into the infested water and crossed over.

After reaching the island's high ground, he cleared a circular area under the tall holly tree, gathered sticks, and built a fire. Adding leaves caused thick, white smoke to swirl up through the trees to be seen from a distance. He wanted to make certain that Smith knew his general location.

He left the island, leaving a plain trail for his enemy to follow. Elmer stated in the note that the cases would be left under the holly tree on Snake Island, but he wasn't going to make it that easy for his tormentor.

But suppose Smith had entered the swamp near Miss Mollie's place? Where would the man be now? Elmer knew he would have to be extremely careful, for anyone could be behind him or up ahead. Why hadn't he considered that possibility before? He'd been so sure Smith would leave the house and go directly to the swamp that he'd not given the matter further thought.

Elmer stopped to listen, wondering if the sounds he heard belonged to the swamp or to a two-legged invader.

He pushed himself to the limit. There was no time to waste. If Smith were ahead of him, it was already too late.

At a marsh, his feet mired deep in thick, black mud. He picked up one heavy foot and dragged the other forward. The sun dropped lower. He felt glued to the muck.

An hour passed. Elmer fell exhausted to solid ground under a slim pine. All he could think about was that night would engulf the swamp before he reached his destination and that Smith would win. Pulling himself to his feet, it took all his strength to lift the two cases. Stumbling, he plodded on, pushing blindly through a hedge of wild plum bushes.

Later, taking a drink of water, he was conscious of his own foul odor. He wiped the wet handkerchief over his face and continued toward his goal.

He heard things, movements that sounded as if others might be stalking close behind. There were also strange sounds up ahead. Then he couldn't hear anything except the ringing in his ears.

"Where do people go when they die, Poppy?"

It was getting late, so late. Why couldn't he go any faster? Why did his feet feel so heavy? What's that awful smell?

Elmer put down the cases, trying to catch his breath. He felt so tired--worn out--so heavy. How did it get so late so quick? Where was he? He looked around, trying to orient himself.

Lifting the heavy cases, he turned toward the right, finally realizing where he was. Slowly, carefully, he picked his path through the thick, clinging kudzu vines.

Up ahead was the patch of trees he sought. The large pine would offer some protection if they started shooting. His pulse quickened as he raked a clean area on the ground.

Gathering sticks and dry leaves, he built a fire, placed the briefcases nearby, unfolded the blanket on the ground, and sat down. He drank the last of his water and ate the last cracker.

He leaned the shotgun against the tree near him and unsnapped the holster at his side. Throwing more sticks on the fire, he filled his pipe. The howls of wild dogs deep in the swamp reminded him that death was everywhere. A panther somewhere to the east screamed for attention, or warning. Other sounds rumbled in unison all around him.

The sense of urgency he'd suffered over the past few days was no more. His energy had dwindled to nothing. He hoped the rattlers were alive and well. He certainly wasn't going to open the cases to find out.

It was all over except the waiting.

He tried to calm his inner being; halter the anxiety; subdue the rage. He only partly succeeded.

He heard the sound, the almost silent steps a man makes stalking his prey. It was a whisper among the swamp noise at dusk time. Looking off to his left, he saw the form, the outline of a man with a shotgun, enter the kudzu tunnel.

He heard Gus Smith chuckle profanity and laugh. "You old fool. I'll teach you to steal from me!"

Smith took a step forward "I see you brought my property. It's good you did, for I was going to make you pay with pain if you hadn't."

"I said in my note I'd return it if you promised to leave us alone."

"Sure, I'll leave you alone. Know what happened to Jo?"

Elmer reached for the shotgun.

"Stay put!" demanded Smith, taking another step. "I beat the hell out of her, and I left her lying on the floor of your kitchen. If she's still there when I get back, I'm burning down your place with her in it!"

"You got your money and dope back. What else do you want?"

Smith took another step. "I want to see you dead, old man. Did you think returning my money and coke would make up for the trouble you've caused?"

He aimed the shotgun at Elmer."Say 'goodbye,' old man!"

Chapter 26

Elmer waited, holding his breath. Smith cursed and laughed as he approached. A belch of fire exploded skyward from the barrel of Smith's shotgun as the would-be-killer suddenly disappeared from the face of the earth, screaming as he plunged to the bottom of the abandoned well.

The old man rolled up the blanket, kicked dirt on the fire, and picked up the cases. Using the flashlight, he found the deer trail and followed it for almost an hour. He escaped the swamp near an abandoned field and followed the old logging road toward the light at Miss Mollie's house. He hoped she had a pot of coffee on and a few leftover biscuits.

Elmer had never known such a long day.

The headlights caught him squarely in its glare. He put down his load and shaded his eyes.

"Just pick up those cases and come on in," ordered Spark. "No funny stuff with that shotgun, now. I got my pistol pointed at you."

He did as he was told, walking into the glare.

"Elmer, they just drove up a few minutes ago. I had no idea ye was anywhere about. Had I known I'd have warned ye," Miss Mollie called from the porch.

"Shut up," Sam Black told her. "Nobody's going to get hurt here if they do what they're told."

Elmer stepped away from the bright headlights.

"Which one has the money in it?" Spark asked.

"Both," said Elmer.

"Well, bring them over here!" demanded Black.

Elmer carried the cases over and put them on the ground. He noticed Black wore his uniform. A patrol car was parked behind Spark's pickup.

"You take one, and I'll take the other," Spark told the deputy.

"I don't know," said Black. "Maybe I oughta take them both."

"No way," replied Spark, picking up one. "Tell you what. You take that one, I'll take this one, and we'll go straight to my place before we open them."

"All right," said Black. "Neither one will open his until we can do it together, understand?"

Spark laughed. "We've got us a fortune here. Money and cocaine."

"What about Smith?" said Elmer. "What's he going to say about this?"

"Now, that's your problem, ain't it?" said Spark. "You don't think he'll believe you over us, do you?"

"Let's get out of here," said Black. "I'm anxious to see what kind of haul we made."

Elmer watched them turn around and drive up the narrow lane to the dirt road.

He stepped up onto the porch. "Miss Mollie, I sure hope you've got some coffee on."

Following her into the kitchen, he dropped into a chair at the table. "How 'bout some apple pie with that coffee, Elmer?"

"Make it a big slice."

He ate four slices of the pie and would have eaten more had there been any more. He drank two cups of black coffee. "Miss Mollie, you make the best coffee in the world."

She cackled. "Ye be wantin' another cup?"

He nodded. "Just enough to sip on."

"Elmer, ye oughta stay outa them swamps starvin' the way ye do when ye venture there."

She refilled his cup. The green bonnet looked new. "Seems like them folks were mighty anxious to get them boxes ye had."

"Seems like." He stood. "Thanks for the coffee and pie. When you see Elijah, tell him there's a pile of money in the hollow tree. It's for you and him. Tell him it's for that portrait he painted of Spice. I'd like to have it."

"Money? What painting?"

"He'll know what I'm talking about."

The woman followed him out onto the porch. "Ye be bringing that little Spicey gal to see me, Elmer, ye hear? She's a good young'un."

The Dodge car was where he'd left it. He slid under the wheel, his whole body a numbing ache.

He turned onto the dirt road and drove slowly across the wooden bridge, down an isolated pathway under overhanging trees. He saw the pickup. The truck had left the road and plowed through a thicket. The lights were still on. Elmer drove on by.

Turning onto the paved highway leading to Action, he drove three miles down the road when he saw the patrol car. It had cleared a ditch, run through a barbed-wire fence, and stalled in the pasture, the blue emergency lights flashing.

Arriving home, he found Jo sitting at the kitchen table drinking coffee and smoking a cigarette. Swollen blue marks blotched her face. She didn't seem surprised to see him.

It was a long time before either spoke. "I warned him not to go after you," she said. "I told him you'd had enough, that he'd be the one to remain in the swamp."

"The less said about any of this, the better."

She got up and poured him coffee. "I want to know. Did you shoot him?"

"No."

"Then how--"

"The swamp swallowed him."

She tried to smile. "I'm going to get myself straightened out. I mean it. I'm going to get so right and straight that you'll trust me with my daughter."

He grunted. "You've a long ways to go, Jo, before that happens."

"I know. I'll trust you to tell me when I'm fit to be a mother to Spice."

"She'll let you know."

He was sitting on the front porch letting his body soak the morning sun when he saw Spice coming across the cotton field from the direction of the House place. He started to get up and go to her but decided against it. She walked into the yard, her arms folded inside the bib of her overalls. The straw hat sat back on her head.

She sat down on the top step and took a deep breath, looking up at him. Beads of perspiration sparkled off her forehead.

"What are you doing?" he said.

"I'm resting, Poppy."

"Did you walk all the way here by yourself?"

"Sure, I did."

He grunted. "And you didn't tell anyone you were leaving?"

"I sure didn't," she said, spreading her hands. "Don't you know nothing, Poppy? If I told them that, they wouldn't have let me come by myself!"

"Then why did you?"

"'Cause I wanted to be with my poppy!"

"Thank God you're safe."

Spice studied him. "You said there wasn't a God, Poppy."

"I've changed my mind about that."

"Why?"

"Because only the good Lord can make a little green-eyed girl."

She thrust her arms inside the bib, sighing. Cocking her head, she glanced back at him. "Poppy, I already knew that. I knew that way back when I was little."

To every thing there is a season, and a time
to every purpose under the heaven
Ecclesiastes 3:1

A note to our readers

Thank you for spending time with us. We hope your visit has been an enjoyable one.

The staff of GoldenIsle Publishers, Inc. is committed to bringing you some of the best in contemporary, adventure, and historical romance stories by writers who know their craft and instill deep feelings in the characters that bring life to a book.

If you have enjoyed sharing the adventure with the people who moved throughout this novel, write and let us know. Your comments will be forwarded to the authors who constantly strive to entertain their readers with carefully researched and intricately plotted stories.

GoldenIsle Publishers, Inc.
2395 Hawkinsville Hwy
Eastman, GA 31023

The Texas brushland wilderness springs to life under the pen of Don Johnson, a cattleman who owned and operated a ranch in la brasada *bordering the Rio Grande.*

Brasada

In the latter days of the Civil War, a lifeline of the South was made up of wagon trains loaded with cotton bound for the neutral ports of Mexico to avoid the Union blockade. This cotton, traded for gold or hard foreign currency, fueled the hungry looms of Europe, kept the Confederacy solvent, and enriched the merchants of Matamoros, known as the "Baghdad on the Gulf". Mexican outlaws attack and decimate a train, leaving three enlisted men to protect and hide the gold. They take refuge in *la brasada,* a crescent of brushland wilderness where Lance Morgan is determined to build an empire of land and cattle, fighting off thieves, killers and crooked officials. He meets his match in the vivacious Colleen who is a product of the harsh environment.

You may purchase copies of *Brasada* at a 20% discount, postage paid. Complete the coupon below and mail to the publisher.

==

Name_____(4-3)

Address_____

City_____State_____ZIP_____

I am enclosing ($17.56) per copy $_____
GA residents add 6% sales tax ($1.05) $_____
Total amount enclosed $_____
Valid in U.S. only. All orders subject to availability

Use your ___Visa___MasterCard#_____

Exp. Date_____Signature_____

GoldenIsle Publishers, Inc.
2395 Hawkinsville Hwy
Eastman, GA 31023